# THE SILENCE OF TOMORROW

## ALSO BY ANTHONY M. STRONG

**John Decker Series**

Prequel — Soul Catcher

What Vengeance Comes

Cold Sanctuary

Crimson Deep

Grendel's Labyrinth

Whitechapel Rising

Black Tide

Ghost Canyon

Cryptid Quest

Last Resort

Dark Force

**Remnants Series**

The Remnants of Yesterday

The Silence of Tomorrow

**Standalone Books**

The Haunting of Willow House

Crow Song

**Patterson Blake FBI Thriller Series**

(as A.M. Strong with Sonya Sargent)

Prequel — Never Lie to Me

Sister Where Are You

Is She Really Gone

All The Dead Girls

# THE SILENCE OF TOMORROW

## REMNANTS BOOK 2

## ANTHONY M. STRONG

WEST
STREET

West Street Publishing

Cover art and interior design by Bad Dog Media, LLC.

ISBN: 978-1-942207-28-3

*For Tiki and Gidget*
*Still miss you guys!*

# CHAPTER ONE

THE MONSTER WAS WATCHING US. I could sense it in the darkness beyond the streetlamps, lurking in the unlit alley between a four-story apartment block and an office building.

"What's wrong?" Clara gripped my arm, her eyes wide.

"Quiet." I put a finger to my mouth and spoke in a side-whisper. "Keep walking. Don't make any sudden moves."

"Hayden?" She didn't keep quiet, which was so Clara. "You're scaring me."

*Not as much as that creature in the alley will if it goes for us*, I thought. But I didn't say that. Instead, I pulled her along, guiding her past the alley and keeping one eye on the dark slit of an opening.

Ahead of us lay New Haven, or what was left of it in this world. The street was lined with cars. Some parked as if their owners had locked them and walked off into oblivion. Others were abandoned in the middle of the road. The claw marks and broken windshields on some suggested the owners of these vehicles had met a less innocuous fate.

We reached an intersection filled with wrecked cars. A truck lay overturned; the cab smashed beyond recognition. A dragging trail of blood smeared the pavement, leading off into a building on the corner that had once been a restaurant but now looked more like a demolition site.

Clara's breath quickened at the sight.

"It's okay," I said, still lowering my voice. "Whatever happened here is long over."

"I don't think this will ever be over," Clara replied, and in her response, I heard fear mixed with hopelessness. "Why is this happening?"

"Let's not worry about that right now." I led her to the right around the truck and off the main thoroughfare. We wouldn't be any more secure on the narrower streets where danger was less obvious, but it was the only way to reach our destination, a safe house in the Prospect Hill district.

Or at least it would have been, except for the creature that stood in the middle of the street, blocking our path.

It looked like an oversized hairless wolf, with oily dark skin, a bony, angular face, and enough teeth to shred a rhinoceros. But this was no canine that had any right to exist. Hell, it hadn't existed before the day I collapsed on that gas station forecourt—the same day that I met Clara. When I awoke, the world was changed, and monsters were real.

Clara took a faltering step, then came to a halt. A whimper escaped her lips.

The creature made no move. Instead, it looked at us with jet black doleful eyes that masked the ferocity of its demeanor.

A prickle ran up my spine.

"What are we going to do?" Clara glanced my way, then back to the still unmoving creature.

"I don't know."

"Why isn't it doing anything?"

"I don't know," I said again, lacking any better response. "Start backing up. Go slow. No sudden moves."

Clara did as I instructed, and together we began inching backward. I ignored the urge to turn and run, and I suspected Clara was doing the same.

We reached the intersection again.

The creature still hadn't moved.

I breathed a sigh of relief. Whatever it was up to, the beast wasn't interested in us. This almost scared me more. Our previous encounters with these creatures hadn't gone well. Hungry and vicious, they would attack without remorse and didn't give quarter. So why were they holding back now?

It didn't take long to find out.

"Look," Clara said, a faint quiver working its way into her voice. She was staring sideways, past the wrecked truck.

I turned and looked.

We had more company. Another creature had appeared across the intersection. It, too, stood unmoving. When I looked behind us, a third beast blocked that escape route.

That left the way we had come.

Except that the first creature I had spotted, the one we had passed a few minutes earlier, was no longer in the alley. It had sauntered out and now blocked our retreat.

"We walked into a trap," I said. The implications of which were only now dawning on me. Rather than acting on pure instinct, these monsters had worked together to catch us. They had executed a coordinated plan. How smart were these creatures?

"What now?" Clara pressed close to my side. I could feel her trembling. Sense the beat of her heart.

The creatures moved in unison. They rose on their haunches and took a deliberate, yet cautious, step forward. Tightening the noose.

"I think now would be a good time to run," I said, glancing around and summing up our options at the same time.

"Where?" Clara's hand slipped into mine.

"That building." I tilted my head toward a six-story apartment block sitting on the intersection's northwest corner. "The lobby door is open."

"You can't be serious?" Clara's eyes flew wide. "We'll be sitting ducks in there."

"We're sitting ducks out here," I countered. "If we can get to the building, get inside, we might be able to cross all the way through and find a back way out. Draw them in and skirt around the creatures."

"It's too risky."

"It's our only viable option." The creatures were slinking forward again. There was no time to debate the matter. "Do as I say."

"I don't like this," Clara said, but she turned toward the building anyway.

Her body tensed as she prepared to run.

"On three," I whispered. "Run as fast as you can. If we get separated, don't stop. Don't look back. Keep going."

"What if—"

"No ifs. Keep moving regardless. It's your only chance."

She didn't reply, but instead squeezed my hand. She understood.

"One . . ."

The creatures padded forward.

"Two . . ."

The closest one lifted its head and sniffed the air as if it were savoring our scent.

"Three!"

We sprinted forward, weaved around a stalled car and dashed for the open doorway in unison.

# CHAPTER TWO

THE CREATURES, realizing our intent, sprang forward and gave chase, desperate not to lose their quarry.

Clara glanced over her shoulder, her pace slowing as she did so.

"Keep going," I urged, letting her move ahead of me and taking a defensive position at her rear as we closed the gap between ourselves and the building.

"They're gaining on us."

"I know." I could hear the beasts crashing forward now, snarling and yipping among themselves, all pretense of stealth abandoned.

"We're not going to make it."

"Yes, we will." I put an arm around Clara's waist; half pulled, half dragged her the last ten feet to the door, as the closest beast sprang toward us.

"Don't stop," I said, propelling her through the door and dodging sideways as the creature bore down upon me.

It snapped at the air inches from my head and tried to adjust its charge, coming to a skidding halt as I lunged forward, almost falling through the building's wide double doors.

Clara was already running through the lobby.

I slammed the doors behind me, thankful that nothing was blocking them, moments before the second beast arrived.

As I turned to follow her, I heard it slam into the safety glass, which sounded like it had held, at least for now.

"Hurry up." Clara risked a glance over her shoulder. She was almost on the far side of the lobby, approaching another set of doors that probably led out into a rear parking lot.

"I'm coming," I said, then realized my error because the rear entrance wasn't clear.

A grotesque beast, bigger than the others, stepped into view beyond the doors.

It waited there like a spider anticipating a fly.

"Watch out," I screeched, pointing.

Clara turned and saw the creature.

She tried to stop, a scream escaping her lips, as the beast slammed into the doors, sending them crashing open.

It padded into the lobby and eyed her.

"Hayden." She spoke my name with a mixture of hope and sorrow as if she were saying goodbye.

*Not today*, I thought, putting on an extra spurt of speed.

The creature must have realized what I was doing because it tensed, ready to leap.

But not before I closed the gap and dragged Clara sideways as the beast launched itself through the air and landed where she had stood moments before.

"Thanks." Clara was breathing heavily.

"You're welcome." Our easy escape was blocked now. I steered her toward a wide red-carpeted staircase that swept up off the ground floor. With creatures at both doors, there was nowhere to go but up.

"No." Clara pulled back when she realized where I was taking her. "We can't go up there."

"We have no choice." I hustled her along even as the front doors gave way with a crash of broken glass. The lobby would be swarming with hungry beasts in seconds. All with one thing on their mind. Us.

"It's a death sentence. We won't be able to get down again."

"If we stay here, we're already dead." I pushed her up the first flight of stairs. "We'll think of something. We always do."

"Coming into this building was a terrible idea."

"Yeah, well, too late to worry about that now." It wouldn't have been my first choice either, but all our other escape routes had been blocked, and it was better than standing there like statues while the beasts closed in.

We reached the top of the staircase and found ourselves on a mezzanine that overlooked the lobby below. Twin elevators stood across from us. One door was half-open. A woman's white stiletto shoe, absent its owner, sat at the threshold of the elevator car. It reminded me of the Gucci purse sitting alone atop the BMW on the day this hell began . . . the day I first met Clara.

"Where do we go now?" Clara asked, breathless.

I glanced around quickly. Corridors ran off in both directions, no doubt to the second-floor apartments. The electricity was off and long shadows pressed toward us. I spotted a door marked 'stairs' to one side of the elevators. "We keep going up."

"I was afraid you were going to say that."

"Not my first choice either," I said, taking her hand. The beasts were on the stairs below, creeping up as if they sensed we were trapped. "Come on."

We ran for the door.

The lead creature reached the mezzanine as I flung the door wide, and let out a throaty growl of anger when it saw us escaping.

Beyond the door was a concrete staircase that twisted upward through a narrow shaft. I was disappointed to see that they did not extend downward back to the lobby. Not that I really expected them to.

"Do you have a plan for getting out of this building?" Clara asked as we climbed upward.

"Other than trying not to get eaten?" I shot back. From somewhere below came the crash of a door slamming back on its hinges. The creatures were in the stairway with us. That sealed it. There was only one safe direction . . . up.

"Other than that."

"Not really. Kind of playing it by ear."

"Great." Clara was panting. The stairs were steep and narrow.

We reached a landing, ignoring the door, and kept moving. We stood a better chance out in the open on the roof than cornered on a high floor inside the building. There would only be one staircase, and the elevators weren't working. Even if they were, I would be loath to use them.

"Not far now," I said, forcing my legs to keep climbing. Up above, I saw one last landing. The roof access. Below us, the creatures were scrabbling upward, moving faster as they got used to the confined space and steep ascent.

We reached the landing and hurried to the door, slamming into the crash bar.

The door flew wide.

We almost fell through, out into the bright sunlight.

The roof was a flat expanse dotted with air conditioning units, a couple of satellite dishes, and a square concrete structure that probably held the elevator mechanisms.

"This way." I took Clara's hand and led her toward the edge of the roof, beyond which was another building of the same height.

Behind us, the access door banged open.

A beast prowled onto the roof, soon followed by a second one.

"We have to jump," I said, summing up the gap between the buildings.

"Are you kidding me?" Clara glanced over her shoulder at the approaching beasts. "It's at least ten feet."

"It's not that far," I said, looking down at the gap. Six floors below us was a narrow alleyway, much like the one the first beast had been waiting in. It was cluttered with dumpsters.

"I can't do it." Clara tugged away. "We'll never make it."

"You have no choice." I stepped back, walked off ten feet, even as the creatures slinked closer, biding their time.

"Ready?" I glanced sideways at her.

"Not really." Clara's face had turned an ashen shade of white. She was shaking.

"Don't think about it. A few seconds and we'll be safe on the other side." I sprinted forward, making sure Clara was right there alongside me.

The beasts lunged forward. A pack of slathering monsters conjured from the depths of hell.

We reached the edge, took a flying step up onto the low wall surrounding the roof, and launched into empty air.

For a moment we hung in the gap, arms and legs flailing.

The opposite roof, which I had assured Clara was close enough to reach, was anything but. I had made a terrible error.

Little by little we lost altitude, before we plunged down between the buildings.

Clara screamed.

I looked up and saw a beast peering down at us from the increasingly distant roof.

I mouthed a silent apology to Clara. Then I closed my eyes and waited to die . . .

# CHAPTER THREE

"HAYDEN!" My world rocked and shook.

"Wake up." The world shook again.

I opened my eyes, and now I wasn't tumbling into the void between two buildings. I was lying on my cot and Clara was hunched over me, long brunette hair cascading around her shoulders like a shimmering gossamer waterfall. She wore a loose shirt that fell a little above her knees.

"Where are . . ." I struggled to make sense of my surroundings. "What happened?"

"You were having a bad dream."

"Only a dream," I muttered.

"And not a nice one, by the sound of it. You were tossing and turning in your sleep. Moaning." She touched my cheek. A gentle caress that sent a shiver through me. "It woke me up."

"Sorry." The nightmare was still raw, so real I could sense it lurking like an intruder inside my mind.

"Hey, not your fault. Not after all we've been through." Even though there was barely enough room for both of us, Clara climbed into my cot. She slid down and wrapped her arms around me. Her breasts pushed against my bare chest. Warm breath caressed my neck.

"Yeah." It was dark. I was in a small, square room with nothing but our two metal-frame cots and a single chair. Barely more than a cubicle with a window on one side that overlooked a crowded skyline packed with skyscrapers.

"Want to tell me about it?"

"We were being chased through the streets by those . . . those monsters. They trapped us on the roof. We had no choice but to jump. We were about to die. It was so real. Like we were really there. God, it was horrible."

"Try to put it from your mind." Clara's mouth was close to my ear. She ran a hand down over my chest.

"Not as easy as it sounds." I turned my head to look at her. The last few days had been nothing short of a nightmare in their own right. Being chased across the country by mindless crazies and slathering beasts as we made our way to New Haven, following cryptic messages sent to my cell phone. Losing J.T., then losing Emily. That one had been worse. She didn't deserve to die in such a manner, transforming into a crazy right before our eyes. I squeezed my eyes shut at the thought of what I'd had to do. Tears rolled down my cheeks. Then there was Darwin—trapped and alone in a world we had believed to be our own, only to find out that it wasn't—left behind by Brooks and his men. They said it was an accident. That the technology used to move between dimensions wasn't perfect. Sometimes it failed. And now we were here—wherever *here* was—and Darwin was somewhere else. Somewhere much worse. That was less than eight hours ago. It was hard to comprehend. "I let Darwin down."

Her brow furrowed. "We'll find him. First thing in the morning, we'll insist that Brooks and Kellerman take us back."

"Damned right." There was no way I was leaving Darwin in that alternate universe. No way in hell.

"They won't be able to refuse. At least if what they told you is right."

"That I'm their leader?"

Clara nodded. "Yes."

"It still feels wrong. I don't remember being their leader. Their founder. I don't remember One World. Any of it."

"You will. We'll get your memories back."

"Maybe. Or maybe we're still being lied to. We have no proof of anything these people have told us. For all we know, they're the bad guys."

"Is that what your gut is telling you?"

I shrugged. "I really have no idea. I'm so confused."

"Then stop worrying about it. We can't do anything until morning, anyway. Lay here with me."

"Maybe you're right." I closed my eyes and tried to clear my mind, but it continued to whirl. "What about you?"

"Me?"

"Yes. You used to be someone else too. I'm not the only one who doesn't remember this world. Aren't you curious?"

Clara shrugged. "I'm not sure I want to know."

I opened my eyes again, looked at her. "Why not?"

"I'm twenty years old. What must my life have been like here if I let someone wipe my memories and stick me in an alternate reality? How bad must it have been?"

"It might not have—"

"Don't." Clara swallowed hard. "No one with a shred of happiness in their life wants to erase their whole identity and live as someone else in a place that isn't their home."

"We have no idea what the people of this world want," I pointed out.

"Agreed. But I know myself. I might have a head full of fiction created by some evil government—at least if you believe those people out there—but my character, my soul, is still the same. I can feel it. I wouldn't agree to something like that now unless my existence was so miserable I couldn't stand it. I wouldn't have agreed to it then, either."

"That's a lot of conviction."

"It's the truth." Clara nestled into my neck. "It's also how I know that you were always a good man, regardless of what was done to you. I can't decide if Brooks and Kellerman are telling us the truth, but I have no trouble believing that you really are the founder of this group called One World, because I've seen the way you care about those around you."

"Clara . . ."

"Don't get all humble on me." Clara pushed herself up on one elbow, then leaned in and grazed my lips with hers.

The touch was electric. I wrapped my arms around her and returned the kiss, eager to feel something other than fear. For the first time in days, I was at peace.

She broke the kiss off and pulled back, her hand resting gently on my chest. Her eyes glistened. She gave a small sigh. "Whatever happens next, whatever the future has in store, I'm glad that we're going to be facing it together."

"Me too." I pulled her back down, kissed her again.

Afterward, she slipped back down to my side and lay there. For a while, neither of us spoke. Then, after I thought she had fallen back to sleep, she spoke again, her voice soft and low. "Hayden?"

"Yes?"

"If I tell you something, will you promise it won't change things between us?"

"That sounds ominous," I replied, suddenly dreading what she was going to say.

"It's nothing bad."

"Then tell me."

"Promise first."

"Okay. You have my word." I pulled a stray curl of hair away from her face. "I promise."

Clara smiled and stroked my neck. "I think I'm falling in—"

A sharp knock at the door interrupted her.

I cursed the bad timing and pushed myself up. "Who's there?"

"Brooks," came the reply. "Get dressed. I need you to come with me."

# CHAPTER FOUR

"WAIT THERE." I climbed out of the cot, leaving Clara where she was under the covers, and went to the door, wearing only my boxer shorts. When I opened it, Brooks was standing on the other side, dressed in the same uniform as when we first met. I wondered if he had even slept. "What's going on?"

Brooks stepped into the room. He glanced at Clara, then back at me. "We're going to meet an informant who works for the government. They have details about the collapsing worlds. Hard proof of what's really going on. They also have new data we can use to make our jumps back and forth safer and more accurate."

Clara sat up, holding the blanket to her chest. "Does that mean we'll be able to find Darwin more easily?"

Brooks shrugged. "Maybe. It depends on the information we receive."

"Sounds great. What do you need from us?" I asked.

"Kellerman thinks you should tag along. You are the face of One World, after all."

"I don't even remember One World let alone being the face of it."

"Doesn't matter. It will allay our contact's fears. Show her she's doing the right thing by giving us this information. She knows you were sent over. Your presence will prove that we're making progress. Gathering the evidence to expose the government's lies. Blow this wide open."

"Her?" Clara asked.

"Yes. I can't reveal our informant's identity for security reasons, but she sits on the Senate committee that oversees the Multiverse Project, as the government calls it. We need her on our side."

"I have no memory of this." I gestured around the room. "None of it. What if your informant finds out?"

"Don't worry. She knows what they did to you. Memory adjustment is standard procedure for people being sent over."

"Memory adjustment." Clara snorted. "You make it sound so innocuous."

"Hey, I didn't coin the phrase. Actually, I think it sounds rather . . ." Brooks searched for the right word.

"Dystopian?" I volunteered.

"That about sums it up." Brooks grimaced. "At first, when alternate world technology was new, they sent people over without wiping their memories. It didn't go well. The pioneers —seriously, that's what they called them—struggled to accept their new surroundings. Their new life. There were some incidents. That's when the agency in charge of running and maintaining the alternate worlds—these days, it's called the Department of Relocation—realized they had to do something, and quickly. They fast-tracked a new line of research. Put their best minds on it and developed technology that could reprogram the human brain. Erase the old and download a new lifetime of memories."

"That's handy," I said, unable to decide if I was impressed or horrified.

"So, are you in?" Brooks asked.

"Will you help us get Darwin out of that collapsing universe?"

"We still have at least twelve hours before we can jump again."

"That doesn't answer my question," I countered. Colonel Kellerman had told us that it wasn't possible to move between dimensions more than once in any twenty-four-hour period. If we did, he said, it would kill us. I wasn't sure I believed him but couldn't see what reason he would have to lie either.

"There's plenty of time before we're able to go back for your friend, if he's even still alive which I doubt."

Clara let out a small sobbing sound.

Brooks ignored her. "You do this for us, and we'll send a party back for Darwin at the earliest possible opportunity. Deal?"

"Deal." I hoped Brooks wasn't playing me.

"Excellent."

"When are we leaving?"

"Zero-Five-Thirty. Half an hour from now."

I looked sideways at Clara. Her eyes were full of hope. "We'll be ready."

Brooks shook his head. "Not we... You. Clara isn't a part of this. She stays here."

"Like hell, I will." Clara sprang up.

Brooks turned to her. "I understand how you feel, but this has nothing to do with you."

"Really?" Clara's eyes flashed with anger. "After all we've been through, how do you figure that?"

"You're not one of us," Brooks said in a matter-of-fact tone. "You're a Lotto."

"I'm a what?" Clara shook her head.

"It doesn't matter." Brooks took a step back toward the door. His gaze shifted back to me. "Make sure you're ready by zero-five-thirty."

"Hold on a minute." There was no way I was leaving Clara behind. "If I go, so does she."

"It's not up for debate."

"Really?" I stepped forward and gripped Brooks' arm to stop him from leaving. "Aren't I your leader. The one who started this whole thing—whatever that might be."

"You were." Brooks paused. "Before you were captured."

"Then I get to say who goes and who stays."

"Not anymore. Until we get your memories back, assuming we even can, Colonel Kellerman is in charge."

"I don't care about my memories. I care about Clara."

"Be that as it may——"

"We both go, or neither of us goes. Take your pick."

"Well, crap." Brooks looked flustered. "You're as pig-headed now as you were before they wiped you. Guess you can change a man's memories, but you can't change his temperament."

"Looks that way," I said with a smile. "What's your answer?"

"What the hell. You want her along, so be it."

"Thank you."

"Don't thank me yet. I can't guarantee her safety if anything happens."

Clara glared at Brooks. "I can take care of myself."

"I have no doubt." Brooks glanced at his watch. "Now hurry up. We leave in twenty."

# CHAPTER FIVE

THIRTY MINUTES after Brooks interrupted our intimate moment together, Clara and I stepped out of the skyscraper that housed One World's twenty-fourth floor headquarters and ventured for the first time into a surreal reality that was, apparently, our real home.

The street we found ourselves on could have been located anywhere in Manhattan or Boston, Chicago or Detroit. But it wasn't. This was none of those places. The buildings that towered above us were taller. Ultra-modern needles in concrete, glass, and steel that pierced the sky. At intervals, enclosed catwalks ran between the monolithic structures, the walkways suspended many floors above us.

Lower down were gantries that carried long sleek vehicles that looked like futuristic bullet trains. I had seen these the previous evening when looking out over the city.

The sun was rising, but the light struggled to reach between the buildings. At ground level, the streetlamps stayed on, lighting the otherwise gloomy street. This I attributed partly to the sky, which was a dark ashen gray, looking almost like a blanket of thick fog hovering over the city.

Yet it was more like home than I cared to admit. Cars inched past, caught in a snarl of city traffic that was all too familiar. Which made sense. Whoever created the false world where I was a fledgling author and Clara worked in a gas station under the eye of the loathsome Walter, had drawn their inspiration from the landscape around them. The one difference? This city was like New York on steroids. It was even more busy, even at such an early hour of the morning, if that was even possible. The cars inched along, bumper to bumper. Horns blared. Frustrated drivers cursed those in front of them. And the air…

"This place smells wrong," said Clara, walking beside me as we crossed the road weaving through the standstill traffic, toward what looked like the entrance to a subway station. "It smells dirty."

Brooks was walking ahead of us with three men I didn't recognize and one that I did—I vaguely remembered that his name was Colt. All five of them, I noticed, had abandoned their military-style uniforms and now wore civilian clothing. He glanced back over his shoulder. "That would be the pollution."

"We have pollution in our world, too," I said. Only last week—God, that was a lifetime ago—the Western governments had attended the annual World Climate Summit in Helsinki. As usual, there had been a lot of talk, but little concrete action. We would, the media assured us, be drowning in an irreversible climate disaster of our own making if we didn't cut carbon emissions soon.

"For one, that place isn't your world, this is," Brooks said as we reached the opposite sidewalk. "And two, if you think climate change is an issue on the world we found you in, wait until you see this one. Overcrowding, rampant industrialization. Greedy politicians who care more for their pockets than they do for clean air. We have it all. New York City, the real one, not the one you would know from the other side, was lost decades ago to rising sea levels. At least most of it. Manhattan. Queens. The Bronx. All gone. Some of New Jersey survived, though."

"Yay." Clara suppressed a nervous giggle. "New Jersey. Yuck."

"Some things are the same in both worlds." Brooks laughed.

"If New York is gone," Clara sked. "Where are we right now?"

"A hundred miles north-west near the Pennsylvania border. This city doesn't exist in your reality. Too new. It was founded a hundred years ago to house the displaced citizens of the Big Apple."

"What's it called?" I asked.

"Refuge City," Brooks replied. "Hardly a fancy name. Utilitarian."

Colt jumped in. "Because it was built as a refuge for people fleeing the coast. Aesthetics weren't high on the priority list."

"The name works well enough," Brooks said.

"Ok, answer me this," I said, hurrying to draw level with Brooks. "If your world is so awful that the government had to relocate entire cities and then create alternate realities to put people in, why didn't they create a true paradise? Why not make those other worlds so perfect that people would be blissful in them, because I can assure you, the world I lived in was no Heaven on Earth."

"This place around us right now, that's where you come from. The world you call home is the illusion. Well, not really an illusion as such, more like…" Brooks checked himself. "Whatever. Doesn't matter. To answer your question, they did create a paradise of sorts by copying this world and dialing back the problems. But here's the thing. People need to feel comfortable in their surroundings. Even people with erased minds and replaced memories. There can still be bleed through. Ghost memories of their old life. Make a world too perfect—no wars or hunger or strife—and it doesn't feel real to those within it. Then there's the other issue. Give people unlimited leisure and everything they could ever want with no need to earn it, and society goes to hell pretty damned quickly."

"And you know all of this how?" Clara asked.

"Because we've been to a reality where they did that. Made things too perfect. The inhabitants didn't appreciate their surroundings. They messed it all up faster than you would believe. Started fighting among themselves. Squabbling and killing each other to take whatever they didn't already have. Before long, they had turned their paradise into a nightmare worse than the one they went there to escape."

"People never change," Clara said.

"No, they really don't," Brooks replied.

"How many realities are there?" I asked.

"A lot. At least thirty. Maybe more," Brooks answered in a low voice. We were approaching the subway station entrance now. He stopped and turned to us. "No more talk of this. Not while we're on the subway. Too many open ears."

"Sure." I nodded. I looked up at the overhead gantries and their gleaming bullet trains. "Why is there even a subway?"

"And why can't we ride on that?" Clara asked, following my gaze. "It looks comfortable."

"It is," Brooks replied. "But it doesn't go where we need to be."

"That's the downtown hyperloop," Colt said. "Gets you anywhere in the five boroughs that make up the core of the city in the blink of an eye. But it doesn't extend to the outer suburbs or industrial areas. For that, we need the subway. Older and slower."

"And a lot more crowded," Brooks said. "Mass transit at its worst."

"But a quarter the price of a ticket on the loop." Colt glanced skyward. "A real bargain."

"Oh." Apparently, the subway wasn't going to be as shinny as the hyperloop. That was a shame. "Where exactly *are we going?*"

"A warehouse in the Packing District."

"What's the Packing District?" Clara asked.

"You'll see soon enough." Brooks turned and started off again with his men at heel. "Come on. We don't have time to linger."

I exchanged a glance with Clara, and we followed along into the subway station. We crossed an expansive lobby packed with milling commuters. Food vendors operated stalls lining the walls and filling the gaps between thick columns that supported the roof. I saw what looked like a burger joint, a Korean restaurant, a taco stand. Larger stores sold electronics, clothes, and jewelry. One store even sold cars—a sleek black automobile with graceful curving lines standing on a raised dais in the middle of the floor. The lobby looked like a cross between Grand Central Station and a downtown mall.

The air was rife with the aromas of a hundred disparate foods interlaced with stale sweat and the occasional whiff of garbage. Noise was everywhere. A blaring cacophony of shouting voices, jangling music, and a mechanical rumbling that came from deep beneath our feet . . . The trains.

We pushed through the crowds and arrived at a bank of elevators—at least twenty of them—where we came to a halt amid a small throng waiting for the next elevator car to show up.

When it did, Brooks and his men pressed forward, making sure we were close behind, and fought their way inside with little consideration for those around them. The elevator car filled fast with what I estimated to be at least fifty people, way more than would have dared cram into any elevator I had ever seen before.

We stood shoulder to shoulder, barely able to move.

The elevator doors closed.

Then we started downward into the bowels of the earth so fast that my stomach flipped into my mouth.

# CHAPTER SIX

I DON'T KNOW how far down beneath the city the subway tunnels ran but judging by the speed of the elevator and the time it took to drop, they must have been deeper than any subway I had ever ridden—or at least, any I remembered riding.

After waiting for less than a minute, we hopped on a train that glided into the station with a whoosh of air.

The train car was crowded. There was no room to sit down.

After a minute, Clara looked at Brooks. "Back before we left, when you knocked on our bedroom door, you called me a Lotto. What did you mean?"

Brooks pointed toward a paper-slim oblong screen that ran the length of the car above the windows. Upon it was a rolling advertisement for something called the Great Migration. "You we're one of the winners," he said.

"I won that?" Clara looked confused. "What is it?"

"Keep your voice down." Brooks glanced around to see if anyone was paying us any attention.

They weren't.

Brooks continued in hushed tones. "The Great Migration

is a worldwide lottery. It's how most people end up crossing over. You buy a ticket, hope to win. If you do . . . free ride to a better life. At least, that's what they tell you."

"A better life." Now Clara understood. "You mean that collapsing world we were in."

"Yes."

"I won a lottery to be a gas station attendant in middle-of-nowhere Vermont?" Clara pulled a face. "Lucky me."

"I'm sure it was miles better than whatever crappy life you had here." Brooks grimaced. "At least until it started to collapse."

"How many people enter the lottery?" I asked.

"Millions." Brooks shifted his weight to keep balance as the train jerked and started to slow. "All handing over their hard-earned money week after week for the chance of a better life."

"Who gets all that money?" I asked. The amount this lottery brought in must be staggering.

"Who do you think? The few remaining governments. They control the technology via a cabal of politicians who sit on the committee that governs it. Most of them have been on it for decades thanks to bribery and rigged elections."

"Sounds like politicians here are even more corrupt than on my world," I said.

"Goes with the territory," said Colt.

"How many people win this lottery?" Clara asked.

"A handful compared to those who enter. Thousands at a time. The system that maintains the worlds can only handle so many people crossing over in one go. It draws a lot of power."

"Tell me more about this system." I wanted to know how it worked.

"Not here." Brooks shook his head. "Not now. Maybe later."

We were approaching an underground station that looked

identical to the first. Except for the sign attached to the station wall that read: Packing District.

The train came to a halt.

The doors opened and passengers spilled out, fighting past those trying to enter.

"Let's go." Brooks led the way as we exited the carriage and rode another sickeningly fast elevator up to the surface. We made our way outside, emerging into a narrow street that was nothing like the one we had left back downtown.

Here, the air was thick with fumes that caught in the back of our throats. It belched from the vents of dilapidated-looking industrial buildings that stood so close to the road there was barely a sidewalk. Which was why most of the denizens of this neighborhood—men and women wearing drab, filthy clothes stained with the byproducts of whatever was being made in the nearby buildings—crowded into the road. These unfortunate people formed a human tide that only parted when rumbling trucks with enormous wheels trundled past, honking at them to get out of the way. It was like nothing I had ever seen.

Neither had Clara.

"What is this place?" she whispered, staring around her in horror. "It looks like something out of a futuristic horror movie."

"Welcome to the Packing District, my friends." Brooks removed three facemasks from his pocket and handed two of them to Clara and me while the other men donned masks of their own. "You should wear these. They won't be much help, but they're better than nothing."

"Thanks." I could feel the fumes working deep into my lungs. My throat tickled and my eyes burned. In the distance, towering over the lower buildings that now surrounded us, I could see the gleaming spires of the high-rise marvels we had left behind. "What do they do here?" I asked.

"What don't they do?" the man named Colt answered.

"This entire section of the city, twenty-four square miles, is nothing but heavy industry. Factories. Warehouses. Manufacturing plants. Slaughterhouses. If you need or eat it, they probably process it here."

"Why is it so polluted?" Clara asked, almost gagging. "Don't you people have rules about clean air?"

"That depends where you live." Brooks gave her a grim stare. "Out beyond the city there are suburbs filled with folk who have never stepped foot into a place like this . . ."

"Rich folk," Colt added.

"But in the city . . . it's another story. Even downtown you can smell the pollution coming out of the Packing District if the wind is blowing in the right direction."

"Why doesn't anyone fix it?" Clara asked. "Does no one care?"

"They care. At least some of them. The good ones," Brooks said. "But others, powerful people in high places, care more about the dirty money lining their pockets that they do about effecting change. The people running these factories and warehouses make sure that any environmental bill that makes it to a vote doesn't make it past one."

"Not that it matters much," Colt said. "The world is too far gone to save. We've made our bed and now—"

"I hate to end this lively little debate," Brooks said, cutting Colt off. "But we need to get moving or we'll miss our rendezvous."

"How far away is it?" I asked. I didn't relish the thought of spending too much time breathing in the noxious fumes that swirled around us.

"Not far. A warehouse three streets from here." Brooks started walking.

We made our way down the street, pushing through the tight throng of factory workers that milled around. I wondered if we had caught a shift change or if it was always this crowded here.

Soon we turned down a narrow alleyway between two buildings, as empty as the streets around us were bustling, and followed it until we came to a dilapidated brick building with tall windows caked in grime.

Brooks approached a metal door set into the building's wall and rapped three times.

For a moment nothing happened, but then I heard bolts being drawn back. The door opened a crack and the thin, bony face of an older gentleman appeared in the gap. "Who are you? What do you want?"

Brooks answered quickly. "My friends and I are looking for spare parts."

I looked at Clara.

She shrugged.

"Parts for what?" asked the man behind the door.

"A BellMaster 5100. Year 2046 model."

The door opened wider. Apparently, this was a prearranged code. The man moved backward to let us enter. "Come in. Quickly."

"Thank you." Brooks stepped inside.

When the rest of us had entered, the man closed the door and motioned for us to follow him across a vast and empty room toward another door set into the opposite wall. Shafts of weak light filtered through the windows, but not enough for us to see adequately, and more than once I almost tripped on a discarded piece of metal or some other small piece of broken machinery.

"None of you are hot?" the old man asked as we went. He moved fast, apparently having no problem seeing.

"No." said Brooks.

"Hot?" I asked, looking at Brooks.

"He wants to know if we have any electronics on us that can be tracked. Like phones or tablets. Anything that can transmit a signal."

"I see." This was all very cloak and dagger.

"Who exactly are we meeting?" Clara asked, looking around at our surroundings as we reached the other door.

Brooks didn't answer. Instead, he turned and looked between Clara and me. "From here on, you keep your mouths shut and only speak when necessary. Got it?"

"You're the one who wanted us along on this less than pleasant jaunt," I reminded him.

Brooks jerked a thumb at Clara. "I wanted you along, not her."

"Too bad," she replied, glaring at him.

Brooks turned his attention to me. "Stick by my side. If anyone speaks to you, try and sound like the leader you're supposed to be."

"I'll do my best." *If only to get back to Darwin*, I thought.

"Good. I'll handle most of the talking, so you should be fine." Brooks turned back to the door, opened it, and stepped over the threshold.

His men were next, followed by the old man.

That left me and Clara.

"After you," I said, gesturing for her to enter.

"Thanks," she replied. "For the record, this whole thing feels wrong. We should watch our backs in there."

"Goes without saying," I said grimly. There were no crazies or monstrous creatures in this world, so far as I was aware, but I wasn't sure if that made me feel any safer.

# CHAPTER SEVEN

THE WAREHOUSE SPACE beyond the door was large, windowless, and dark save for a row of grimy skylights set high in the ceiling that cast long poles of drab illumination down onto the scarred and oily concrete floor.

Clara moved close to me as we stepped away from the door and further into the gloom.

A few feet ahead of us, Brooks and his men were advancing with caution, looking left and right as they moved toward the center of the warehouse. The old guy who had met us at the front entrance walked off to one side with a shuffling gait.

A prickle of apprehension surged up my spine, but I could not place the source of my nervousness. After all, I was a writer, not a soldier. At least, so far as I remembered.

"Look sharp," Brooks said to his men, picking up on the same unease. He glanced toward our guide and motioned for us all to halt. "I think this is far enough in for me. Where's our contact?"

"She's here. Waiting. We had to make sure of who we were meeting." The old man licked his lips and shuffled from one foot to the other. His gaze turned from Brooks to me. "I'll go tell her it's safe to come out."

"Not alone, you won't." Colt said quickly. He turned to Brooks. I'll go with him. Make sure the senator really is here."

"Good idea." Brooks motioned to one of his other men. "Dansk. Go with them."

Dansk nodded and stepped forward.

"You don't trust me, eh?" The old man squinted at Brooks.

"I don't trust anyone but myself and my men."

"Suit yourself." The old man shrugged. He started off into the darkness, with Colt and Dansk trailing behind. Soon they were lost to the gloom, then even their footfalls were gone.

We stood in silence and waited.

Somewhere off to our right, I heard a steady drip of water. Above them, high in the building's rafters, came a flap of wings as a bird took flight.

A couple of minutes ticked by.

"Where are they?" I asked, moving closer to Brooks. "This is taking too long."

"Patience," Brooks replied, but I could hear the strain in his voice.

"Wait. I hear someone now." Clara touched me on the shoulder.

And now I heard them as well. Light footfalls echoed through the cavernous building. One set, getting closer.

A lone figure appeared. Diminutive. A woman in her forties with auburn hair tied back in a tight bun against the back of her head. Her face was gaunt, eyes narrow. She kept her gaze fixed on us as she approached; the shadows falling off her like mist burning away in the morning sunlight.

When she drew within ten feet, she stopped in a shaft of light from one of the overhead windows and lowered the mask she was wearing to combat the thick, polluted air of the Packing District.

"Jason Brooks. Good to see you again."

"Good to see you too, Senator Kane." Brooks made no attempt to move closer. "You look well."

"I look like someone with the weight of worlds on my shoulders but thank you anyway." The Senator shifted her gaze to me. "My goodness. It really is him."

"Yes." Brooks nodded. He kept his own mask in place.

"How…" The Senator paused and looked back at Brooks. "How did you locate him?"

"It wasn't easy." Brooks was being cagey. "But we have our ways."

"I wasn't sure if I believed it when I heard the news. He was buried so deep into an older world. Frankly, I'm surprised the place lasted long enough for you to mount an extraction. He was supposed to disappear quietly. Go down with the ship, so to speak."

"As I said, it took a lot of resources," Brooks said.

"You know, there was even a cover story ready for the possibility that the collapsing world was discovered, unlikely as that scenario was. you would have been the scapegoats. Terrorists who found a way to destroy an entire reality, accidentally killing their own leader. It would be an easy sell given your name. *One World.*"

"I have no doubt." If this admission phased Brooks, he didn't show it.

"So now the question becomes, what are you planning to do with him next?"

"I think it's better if you don't know the specifics."

"Of course." The senator smiled. "He doesn't have his genuine memories, I assume?"

Brooks shook his head.

"I see."

"We'll get them back."

"Maybe. Or maybe you won't. Either way, Hayden Stone reappearing like this will present a real problem for those who wish to keep the status quo. Memories or not, he knows too much. There's a lot at stake here."

"I'm aware of that, which is why we need the proof you brought to us. With solid evidence of the government's deceit and the firsthand testimony of Hayden Stone, we can finally do some good."

"Yes. The evidence." A look of sadness flashed across the senator's face, only to vanish as quickly. "How long have we known each other, Jason?"

"A long time."

"And you trust me?" The senator removed a small oblong object from her pocket that looked like a tiny thumb drive. She turned it over in her palm.

"You know that I do." Brooks stepped forward and reached for the drive.

"Perhaps you shouldn't have." The senator slipped the drive back into her pocket.

I looked at Clara. My unease about this situation had been valid. I was also aware that Colt and Dansk had not returned with the senator.

"What are you doing, Senator?" Brooks asked, without a trace of alarm in his voice. Had he suspected a double-cross? I didn't think it was likely given the way we walked in here. Maybe he was just a good tactician, unwilling to show weakness.

"I'm protecting my family . . . and myself." The senator closed her eyes for a moment. Opened them again. A tear rolled down her cheek. "I'm so sorry, Jason. They found out about me. Offered me a deal. This was the only way."

"Giving up the people you've been working with for years? Betraying your friends? I thought you had more morals than this." Brooks retreated toward me and Clara. His remaining men huddled close and looked around warily.

"Morals aren't any good to a dead woman." The senator wiped the tear away.

"They'll kill you anyway," Brooks said. "Right after they get what they want."

"I doubt it. I took precautions long ago. I know too much for them to do that, at least if they get all of you." Her eyes flicked to me. "And if they can neutralize Hayden Stone once and for all. Oh, I'm sure I'll be persona non grata in certain circles for a while, but this is politics. It's not what you already did that matters, it's who you choose when push comes to shove."

"You're more useful as a grudging servant than a dead enemy."

"Something like that." The senator glanced back over her shoulder. "I think we're done here."

A figure stepped out of the darkness. A burly man wearing army fatigues but no insignia. And at his side, padded an immense beast. One of the creatures from the collapsing world that I still thought of as my true home.

Clara shrank back.

"Where did you get that?" Brooks stood his ground.

"You're not the only one who's been taking little jaunts between worlds and bringing things back." The senator looked toward the creature, and in her eyes, I saw revulsion . . . and fear. "They tell me this one is tame . . . sort of. An implant that channels its urges."

"You've got to be kidding me." Brooks shook his head.

"I wish that I were. This wouldn't have been my go-to method of killing you all, but certain people thought it would be poetic."

"And how will you explain the corpses when we're found?"

"What makes you think anyone will find your bodies?"

Brooks met the senator's gaze. "You don't have to do this, Senator. There's still time."

"No, there isn't. Not for you. It's nothing personal, Jason. I hope you know that. If there were any other way..." The senator cast one more glance at the beast, pulled her mask back up, and then turned and walked away. The soldier at her side watched us a moment longer, and then followed. Soon they were both swallowed up by the gloom, before even their footsteps, ringing on the concrete floor, could no longer be heard. Which meant we were alone with the beast.

# CHAPTER EIGHT

"Stay behind me." Brooks placed himself in front of us while his remaining two men took up positions to his left and right. None of them were armed. which was, in hindsight, a bad tactical error.

The creature hadn't moved. Perhaps it was waiting to be released from whatever inhibitor the senator and her goons were using to control it, or maybe it was savoring the moment. I knew the creature was smart from previous encounters with its kind.

"We have to run," Clara said, her voice reedy and thin with stress. She glanced toward the open doorway behind us. "That creature will rip us apart."

"Running won't help. If anything, it will make us easier targets. You can't fight with your back turned." Brooks never took his eyes off the beast. "Stay right where you are and have a little faith."

Faith. I wasn't sure we should be relying on such an abstract concept given the situation. I was about to say as much, when the beast let out a rumbling, low growl and took a small step forward.

"Hayden…" Clara gripped my arm. Her fingers dug into

my flesh through the fabric of my shirt. I could almost feel her heart slamming against her ribs.

"It's going to be okay," I said, hoping that Brooks knew what he was doing.

No sooner had I uttered the words, than the beast took another more forceful step forward, then hunkered down, hackles rising.

Then it launched itself toward us.

A shot rang out, followed by another.

The creature pivoted midair and tumbled off into the gloom with an angry squeal.

I looked around, startled, and saw a silhouetted shape high up on a gantry above the warehouse floor. The figure held what could only be a high-velocity rifle. When I looked the other way, I saw another figure on the opposite gantry. Brooks hadn't come unarmed and vulnerable after all. I sagged with relief.

Until the creature reappeared, a little more cautious, but still very much alive.

"That's not good." Clara tensed next to me. Her hand slipped from my arm and found mine. She gripped it.

I knew she wanted to run, was doing her best to resist the urge.

Brooks glanced our way. "This is going to get ugly. When I tell you to, make a dash for the door."

"What about you?" I kept a wary eye on the beast, which was returning the favor. For now, at least, it was content to sum up the situation lest it end up on the receiving end of another rifle shot or two.

"Don't worry about us." Brooks lifted his head toward the men on the gantry. "We'll keep the beast occupied. Won't be the first time."

"I don't like this." I might not remember being the leader of this group, but my sense of duty told me not to abandon them.

Brooks must have read my mind. "Listen to me, Hayden. You need to stay alive if we have any hope of getting the truth out. Getting yourself torn apart in this warehouse won't do any of us a lick of good."

"But…"

My protest was cut off. "And you need to keep Clara safe. You insisted that she come along. She's your responsibility."

"Brooks…"

"My men will take care of the creature."

I fell silent, knowing that further argument would only waste valuable seconds.

"You ready?" Brooks asked.

I nodded.

"Good. Get back to headquarters quick as you can. Stay off the subway. Tell them what happened here."

The beast crept forward, emboldened now.

"Okay." I nodded again.

"With any luck, I'll see you soon." Brooks took a deep breath. He raised his hand.

The beast slouched down, preparing to strike a second time.

Brooks brought his arm down in a chopping motion. A signal to his men on the gantry. At the same time, he hissed, "Both of you . . . run."

Then all hell broke loose.

# CHAPTER NINE

THE BEAST LUNGED FORWARD, landing among us with a guttural growl. Brooks rolled to the left and barely avoided the creature's gnashing jaws while his remaining men scattered like a set of pins hit by a well-placed bowling ball. Clara stumbled backwards with a frantic scream.

I saw one of the men on the gantry toss a weapon down toward one of the men flanking Brooks. A snub-nosed gun that looked a little like the semi-automatic weapons I had seen in action flicks. Not that I knew anything about guns like that, or at least, if I did, that information was locked behind a firewall of engineered amnesia overlaid with my *struggling author* personality.

The man caught the gun as Brooks reached for a second one thrown by the man on the opposite gantry.

No one sent anything my way, and I had no intention of sticking around unarmed to fight the beast with my bare hands.

"Come on," I said, retreating toward Clara and tugging at her arm.

She didn't need any encouragement.

Together we sprinted for the door, reaching it as a volley of deafening gunfire erupted. I cast a glance back toward the melee as we fell through the opening and caught a glimpse of Brooks standing legs apart, weapon held in both hands as it spat a hail of deadly fire toward the beast. Or at least it would have been deadly for any other animal. This creature was built like an armored car, its thick scaly hide barely even scratched by the volley of slugs. All the assault managed to do was drive the enraged monster back into the gloom.

From above more gunfire erupted as the men on the gantry joined in now that the beast was far enough away that they wouldn't end up shooting their comrades.

Then my view of the confrontation was cut off as I moved away from the door.

"We can't leave those men behind," Clara said, stopping now that we were clear of the inner warehouse.

"I don't think we have much choice." We weren't armed and judging by the chatter of gunfire Brooks and his men were holding their own. I got her moving again and we headed across the warehouse toward the street.

"We could have been killed back there," Clara said, breathless, as we went. "That senator woman lured us into a trap."

"I know." Brooks had trusted the senator. Believed she was on our side. One of the good ones. Instead, they had gotten to her . . . whoever *they* were. I scoured my mind for any trace of a memory that would tell me how I knew the woman, because she knew me. But I came up blank. I was the same Hayden Stone who had wandered into that gas station off I-89, who remembered writing a book, and getting a publishing deal. A man with a brother called Jeff who was having a baby with his beautiful wife. That life, the one where I was living in Vermont and liked to eat Chinese food on Friday nights and go to Mulligan's Bar with my friends on Saturdays . . . that was my reality.

Still, the look on Senator Kane's face when she saw me. That wasn't fake. Which meant Brooks was telling the truth. Crazy as it sounded, I was the leader of a resistance movement trying to expose a deadly secret that the government of this world would stop at nothing to keep that way. Even if it meant killing people with a mutated beast from a shattered reality.

We reached the door leading to the street.

Clara was about to step through when I stopped her.

"What?" She turned and looked at me.

"I'll go first. We don't know if there are people waiting for us out there, covering the exits to make sure no one escapes that beast."

"And what if there are?" A look of panic flashed across Clara's face. "They could kill you."

"I know." The thought had occurred to me, but what choice did we have? It was either that or huddle in the warehouse and hope Brooks and his men could take down the beast before it ripped them apart and came looking for fresh meat. I could still hear bursts of muted gunfire from back the way we had come, which meant the creature was busy for now, but how long would it stay that way?

"We should look for another way out."

"There isn't time," I replied. "And even if we found one, it wouldn't be any safer."

"I hate this," Clara said.

"Me too," I agreed, then stepped through the door and out onto the street before my nerves got the better of me.

# CHAPTER TEN

THE ALLEY WAS EMPTY.

That didn't mean we were safe. I'd seen enough movies to know that a sniper could be lying in wait anywhere. A rooftop. One of the windows in the building opposite. There were a hundred places a gunman could conceal themselves.

One crack of a rifle, and I'd be down before my brain even registered what was happening. But there was no bullet waiting for me on the other side of the door. No marksman with me in his sights. The alleyway was as it appeared. Which meant one of two things. Either the senator and her cronies were lax in planning their trap, or they were convinced the beast they unleashed against us would do the job. Or maybe there was another reason. They didn't care if we escaped, because they knew we had no proof without the senator's cooperation. Maybe they wanted to see if I really was alive and back in the real world. But that last one left me feeling uneasy. I was missing something.

"Is it safe?" Clara was standing in the doorway. She glanced over her shoulder toward the inner door where a faint pop of gunfire could still be heard, less frequent now.

"Yes." I motioned for her to come out. I could feel the

Packing District's noxious fumes burning the back of my throat now that we were outside again, despite the mask that I still wore.

Clara stepped into the alley and closed the door, further muffling the gunfire. She coughed and rubbed her eyes. "This feels too easy."

"Tell me about it." As she joined me, a horrible thought flashed through my mind. What if there really was a gunman, and he was waiting for Clara to make an appearance before taking his shot. A good sniper would make sure to acquire all their targets before playing their hand. But as the seconds ticked by, I realized my fears were unfounded.

"We should wait and see if Brooks and his men make it out."

"No." I shook my head. "He ordered us back to their headquarters, and that's what we must do. Lingering here won't help anyone, and they know their own way back."

"Do *we*, though?" Clara asked, looking down the alley.

"We'll find it." I looked up at the imposing skyline dominating the horizon. Somewhere in that mass of buildings was the skyscraper we had left not more than ninety minutes before. How long it would take us to get back there, I had no idea. I took Clara's hand. "Come on."

We hurried from the alley and onto the street where we turned left toward downtown. When we reached the subway entrance, Clara turned to enter, but I stopped her. "Not there. Remember what Brooks said."

"How else are we going to get all the way across town?"

"The old-fashioned way. On foot."

"That's going to take hours. It must be miles away."

"I know."

"Then screw Brooks. Let's take the subway."

"No. He must have had a good reason for wanting to keep us out of the subway." I suspected I knew why. Now that the senator and whoever she reported to knew I was alive, my face would be a liability. Even back on the simulated Earth I called home, there were facial recognition systems and high-definition cameras everywhere. Some of the most sophisticated, like those used at airports, could recognize a person with such efficiency that they could pass through security or board a flight without any interaction with TSA or gate personnel. By extension, it could also flag criminals and those on watchlists. Even Vegas used it to track and intercept cheaters before they ever reached a poker table. How much better would the technology be in a world like this? But there was another, more mundane reason to avoid the subway. "Even if we wanted to, we can't. We don't have any money to pay the fare. Brooks took care of it on the way here."

"Damn. I never thought of that."

"Also means that hailing a cab is out, assuming they even have such a thing on this world."

"Double damn." Clara scowled. "I've done enough walking in the last week to last a lifetime."

"Yeah." I couldn't argue with that. "At least there aren't any crazies around here."

"That we know of." Clara followed me past the subway entrance, weaving through the bustling crowd of dour-faced workers that clogged the street. "An hour ago, I thought there were no beasts either."

"If whoever brought it here was smart, they only grabbed the one." Except that even bringing a single creature to this world was a bad idea. If it got loose to run uncontrolled through the city it would wreak havoc, killing everyone in its way until it could be brought down. Worse, there would be panic far and wide. I was fairly sure the general population had no idea such creatures existed.

We continued on foot, heading in the general direction of downtown, and doing our best not to attract undue attention. I couldn't help wondering about Brooks and his men back at the warehouse. Had the beast killed them all? I was certain the pair Brooks sent along with the old man, Colt and Dansk, had either been arrested or met an untimely end before the senator even made her appearance. I hoped it was the former. But what about the others?

I pushed the thoughts from my mind. There was nothing I could do for them, and we had our own worries. Like finding our way through a strange and unfamiliar city under the threat of being recognized and dragged off to an uncertain fate by a corrupt government who viewed me and those close to me as the enemy. Which was laughable considering I didn't even remember this world or any of its inhabitants.

But none of that mattered. Right now, all I wanted to do was get back to the skyscraper that contained the world-hopping technology required to rescue Darwin and keep Clara safe as we did so. Everything else was noise.

# CHAPTER ELEVEN

THE CITY STRETCHED ON FOREVER. We left the Packing District behind after walking for almost thirty minutes and entered into an area dominated by what I assumed were apartment buildings that rose ten or more floors up into the ashen sky. Each one looked like the next. Drab concrete boxes crowded next to each other with barely a space between them.

Garbage cans overflowed in the narrow alleys between the buildings. When the wind kicked up their smell assaulted our nostrils. A noxious odor of rotting food waste mixed with what I could only assume was the malodor of raw sewage drifting up through metal grates from the sewers beneath the road. Children played on the stoops, seemingly oblivious to the stench. Men and women leaned in doorways and watched us pass by; faces wrought with the hardship of their lives.

This was, I realized, the place where all those workers clogging the streets of the Packing District must live. A slum devoted to housing the lowest levels of society.

"God, what a dreadful way to exist," Clara said, looking around in horror.

"I bet there are similar places on our world," I said, realizing as I uttered the words that technically *this* was our world and the other nothing but a cleverly crafted illusion.

"Do you think I was in a place like this?" Clara asked with a shudder. "Before my name was drawn in that crazy lottery and I ended up working in a gas station with my memories erased."

"I'm sure your situation wasn't great," I replied. "Otherwise, why would you enter."

"Good point." Clara fell silent for a moment, as if she were thinking. "What are we going to do?"

"First, we're going to find Darwin."

"No. I mean after that," Clara said. "How are we going to survive long term in this world without being arrested . . . or killed. You are enemy number one if that senator is to be believed. They tried to kill us back at the warehouse. Next time they might succeed."

"Let's worry about that when the time comes," I said, because I didn't have an easy answer.

"I think we should worry about it right now." Clara glanced around, her eyes darting from one building to the next. "It will be impossible to hide forever. We could be spotted at any time. And I don't hold out much hope that One World have the resources to win this fight given what we've seen of them so far."

"All I'm concerned with at this moment is making it back to One World's headquarters in one piece. After that, we can make plans. Figure out how to move forward."

"This is a nightmare," Clara said. "It's almost worse than our previous situation."

I shrugged. "At least we're alive."

"For now." Clara looked at me and I saw fear in her eyes. "Maybe we shouldn't go back to that skyscraper."

"I don't think we have much choice given the circumstances."

"I'm serious. Think about it. That senator lured us into a

trap back there. How do we know it's even safe to go back to One World's headquarters? If they know we escaped, they might be waiting for us."

"We don't." I had already thought of that. The ephemeral they—I wasn't sure exactly who *they* were or how many people were involved with the exception of the senator—were intent upon silencing One World, and by extension myself. It would be easy to lay in wait for us, figuring we would return to the only place we knew. We could be walking into a worse trap than the one we had escaped. But what other choice was there? I said as much, then added, "We won't survive long on the streets without money or transportation. We need One World, maybe more than they need us. At least for now."

"But—" Clara started to object. She was too smart for her own good sometimes.

"No buts. It's a risk we have to take. Besides, this is the only way I know to get Darwin back."

"You're right, of course," admitted Clara, but I could tell she wasn't happy.

"I'm always right." I forced a grin, hoping to inject a little levity into the situation, but it rang hollow.

Clara observed me for a moment then turned her attention back frontward. "This is taking forever."

"We're almost out of the slum." I could see a bridge up ahead, crossing a swollen and fast flowing river. It reminded me of the Golden Gate Bridge, painted as it was a rusty red, except that it was at least twice as long, and the cables holding it suspended above the roiling waters looked like they could survive a ten on the Richter scale without so much as a tremble. I wondered what kind of foul weather this planet experienced that it was so seemingly over-engineered.

"Thank goodness." Clara picked up her step. "I hate this place."

# CHAPTER TWELVE

WE CROSSED the bridge via a narrow pedestrian walkway that flanked the main carriageway into the heart of the city. We were not the only travelers using foot power to get from one side to the other. A steady stream of people trudged out of the slum toward the gleaming spires of downtown. At times the traffic beside us became so snarled that we overtook vehicles as they sat trapped in a creeping line. I wondered if this was why we had ridden the subway to our meeting with the senator. The congestion in this city was bordering on a parking lot and the bridge, being one of the only routes from downtown, clearly acted as a bottleneck for it all.

A hundred feet below, flowing under us, was a dirty brown river that reminded me of pictures I'd seen online of the polluted Yamuna, a tributary of the Ganges River. I saw trash floating by. Lots of it. While most was unidentifiable, at least once I saw an object that had a vaguely human shape. A shiver ran up my spine and I forced my gaze away from the nasty soup of waste and water flowing under us.

Clara walked at my side, and I noticed she too was averting her gaze from what lay beneath. If she saw the body floating by, she said nothing, and I didn't bring the matter up.

Soon after, we exited the bridge and found ourselves amid the high-rise buildings that made up the core of this city.

I stopped on the sidewalk and looked around. Other pedestrians milled past me like a parting wave.

"What's wrong?" asked Clara.

"Trying to get my bearings." I had no idea how to get back to the building we'd left hours earlier with Brooks and his men. All I remembered was the name of the subway station opposite because I saw it as we entered. "The subway stop was called Broadbend Row. If we can get back there, the building we need is on the opposite side of the street."

"Let's ask someone." Clara stepped in front of a man wearing blue coveralls and carrying what looked like a metal lunch box. But before she could speak, he scowled and dodged her.

"That went well," I said.

"If at first you don't succeed..." Clara approached a second pedestrian. This time she chose a woman. As before, the pedestrian tried to skirt around her, but Clara persisted. "Wait. My friend and I are lost. We need directions."

The woman hesitated, then stopped. "Okay but make it quick. If I'm late for work, I'll end up fired."

"Broadbend Row," I said, stepping in. "It's a subway station."

"I know what it is." The woman pointed down the street. "Keep going this way for eight, maybe ten blocks. Look for 17th Avenue North. When you get there, turn left and go one block over then turn right. Broadbend will be there."

"Thank you." Clara looked relieved.

"You look kind of familiar." The woman studied me with narrowed eyes.

A tingle worked its way up my spine. "I have that kind of face."

The woman observed me for a moment longer, then turned and walked off with a shrug.

"What was that about?" Clara asked.

"Beats me," I replied even though I had my suspicions. "We should get moving. I have a feeling the quicker we're off the streets, the better."

# CHAPTER THIRTEEN

IT TURNED out to be twelve blocks.

We moved at a brisk pace and kept our heads down. I was feeling paranoid now. The woman who gave us directions might really have thought I looked a bit like her friend's brother, or that I resembled some guy she knew at a job years before. A face she had half-forgot but still lingered at the back of her subconscious.

Or she might have seen me on the news at some point in the past. The leader of a troublesome fringe group pushing what I was sure the powers that be must have labeled conspiracy theories.

If that were the case, then my paranoia was justified. We were supposed to have died in that warehouse. We couldn't risk being recognized. Couldn't take the chance that news of our survival would reach the people who tried to kill us. If that happened, they would come after us again.

No, not us. Me.

It was my forgotten past that was putting Clara in mortal danger. If I were not with her, she could have simply reintegrated into society, and nobody would even know she had returned from a collapsing alternate reality.

For a wild moment I considered telling her we should split up, that she would be safer on her own. But one look at Clara's face told me she had anticipated this thought.

She confirmed it a moment later.

"Not happening," she said, shaking her head. "We stick together."

"You don't even know—"

"I could see it on your face. You were about to suggest we go our separate ways. You think you're a liability to me."

"I am a liability. I almost got you killed back in that warehouse."

"No." Clara's voice was hard. Definitive. "That bitch of a senator almost got both of us killed. That creature she released probably did kill Brooks, Colt, and the others. Don't even think of blaming yourself for being part of something you don't even remember."

I knew when I was beaten so I didn't press the matter further. Plus, she was right. But there was something else too. I didn't *want* to leave Clara, watch her walk away and disappear into the crowd. We had grown close in the short time since we'd met at that gas station in Vermont on the day everything went to hell. After all we'd been through, after all we'd lost, I didn't want to lose anyone else. Especially not her. Not Clara.

So I kept quiet and walked beside her until we reached 17th Avenue North. And then, a few minutes later, there it was in front of us. Broadbend Row. And opposite the subway station entrance, on the other side of the street was the building that contained the headquarters of One World.

A rush of relief washed over me as we hurried down the street under the shadow of the gantries that held the hyper-loop. A train whisked by with a quiet whoosh.

As we drew close, I looked up at the gleaming skyscraper. Many floors above us, the technology to save Darwin was waiting. We would jump across to the reality Brooks and his men had found us in and bring him back to a world that wasn't collapsing, then get the hell out of Dodge, as the expression went. Find somewhere safe to live out the rest of our lives, if there was such a place.

"Wait." Clara put a hand on my arm as we drew close.

"What is it?" I came to a stop and looked at her.

"I don't know." She shook her head. "I think we should be careful. We might be walking into another trap."

"We've been through this already." I understood her concern, but the only way to know, was to go up there and see. It was a risk, for sure, but a necessary one. "We agreed to risk it."

"I'm having second thoughts." Clara squinted up toward the towering monolith. "I think I should go up first. No one knows who I am. If it's safe, I'll come back down and get you."

"I don't like that idea," I told her, but I knew it made sense. Clara was another face in the crowd. There must be a hundred businesses calling that skyscraper home. One World occupied one floor. Maybe not even *all* of one floor. If the authorities were waiting for us . . . for me . . . she could find out. It would be easy. So why did I feel so unsure about the plan? I didn't have a good answer, so in the end I said, "Fine. Go check it out. But get out of there at the first sign that anything is amiss."

"I will, of course." She nodded.

"Sure wish we had a couple of cell phones," I said. "It would make this so much easier."

"Well, we don't." Clara squeezed my arm. "Don't worry. I'll be fine, and you're probably right. There won't be any goons up there waiting for us."

"Be careful."

"I will." Clara let go of my arm. She followed the sidewalk toward the building, another nameless worker heading to her mundane corporate job as far as anyone else was concerned.

I stepped into a doorway, looking to make myself invisible.

Clara reached the skyscraper. She disappeared inside.

I leaned against the wall, watched the cars crawl along. This world was always stuck at rush hour.

A disheveled man with wild hair and dirty clothing stumbled along the sidewalk. He stopped and observed me. I noticed that his hands shook as he held them to his sides. He was obviously homeless, and probably spaced out on some drug or other. I wondered if he was going to ask me for food or money, but instead his gaze drifted away from me, and he carried on his way.

I watched him go into the subway station then turned my attention back to the doorway Clara had entered.

At that moment there was an ear-splitting boom and the side of the building that housed One World's headquarters disintegrated in a ball of flames.

# CHAPTER FOURTEEN

I TURNED to shield myself as a blast tore through the upper floors of the building, sending shattered glass and twisted steel raining down upon the street. A wave of searing heat washed over me. People on the exposed sidewalk screamed and ran for cover. Cars and trucks skidded to a halt to avoid falling debris. Some vehicles didn't react in time and hit those ahead of them. Likewise, more vehicles yet piled on behind. The hyperloop had taken a direct hit and was missing a good portion of its gantry. The next train that came around would have a hell of a surprise. But that wasn't my problem.

I looked up toward the damaged building. Orange fire licked around a gaping hole in its side below one of the slender walkways that linked it to another skyscraper high above the street. Acrid black smoke poured into the sky.

Another rumble echoed from deep within the building, followed by a fresh belch of flames. A secondary explosion.

"Clara," I gasped. She was somewhere inside that destroyed building. Was she in an elevator when the explosion hit? An image of elevator cars plunging down a ruined shaft, their cables severed, filled my head. I banished the thought, prayed that she had already stepped out of the elevator. But was that any better? I couldn't tell from which floor the explosion had originated, but one thing was clear. One World's headquarters were gone. Was Clara already there when it happened? I had to find out.

The falling wreckage had abated now. Smaller, lighter items fluttered down. Pieces of scorched paper. The remains of a blouse, white with rusty red splotches that could only be one thing. What color top was Clara wearing? I realized I couldn't remember. But it wasn't a blouse.

I stepped out from the doorway, glancing skyward to make sure nothing with enough heft to maim was hurtling down toward me, and then picked my way across the road. I navigated around destroyed cars, their roofs caved in, and chunks of mangled steel that had lived ten floors up only moments ago.

I saw a man lying face down on the ground in a widening pool of blood. He was clearly dead.

A woman's red purse sat discarded and alone on the sidewalk. It reminded me of a similar purse sitting atop a car back at the gas station on the day this all began. It taunted me. A portent of things to come? One red purse on the day I met Clara, and now another on the day I lost her.

"Stop it," I said aloud, chiding myself. "You don't know that she's dead."

*You don't know that she's not*, came the silent reply inside my head.

Only one way to find out.

I reached the entrance to the building. The glass frontage was gone, shattered when the blast hit. Small crystalline pebbles crunched underfoot when I entered the ruined lobby.

A woman in a charcoal suit, her face streaked with blood and soot, stumbled the other way toward the street. Behind her I saw more people crossing the lobby. Men and women of all ages. A throng of survivors escaping the calamity. A couple hundred at least, all rushing for the exits.

I scanned the sea of faces but didn't see Clara. My heart fell.

The stream of evacuees flowed around me as I pushed in the other direction, deeper into the lobby. There weren't as many people as I would have thought given the building's size. How extensive was the damage above? And how many workers were trapped on higher floors, unable to reach ground level?

Another gaggle of survivors appeared, this one smaller than the last. Some were walking under their own steam, while others were being helped. I watched them go with a rising sense of dread. Still no Clara.

Then the power blinked out.

Hardly surprising given the circumstances.

A moment later, dim emergency lighting came on.

I glanced toward the row of elevators. Four shiny aluminum doors set into a wall of richly veined marble. None of them were open, which meant that the cars must have been on higher floors when the blast hit. That didn't automatically mean they had fallen. But then I noticed thin wispy curls wafting around the doors. Even if the cars were still suspended, anyone trapped in them would be asphyxiated if smoke was filling the shafts.

I pushed against the flow of evacuees toward the elevators, reached my palm out toward the metal. Raw heat warmed my palm before I even touched the doors.

There was fire on the other side.

It was worse than I thought.

If Clara was trapped in an elevator, she would already be gone.

I expelled the grim thought from my mind and continued exploring. Above me I heard a cracking sound. A cloud of dust fell from the ceiling.

My gut tightened. Was the entire skyscraper going to come down and bury me? I should leave now. Get out before the worst happened. But not until I had done everything I could to find Clara.

The question was, how?

With the elevators out of action—even if there had still been power and they worked I wouldn't have gotten into one —there was no way to reach the upper floors. But there must be stairs somewhere. There always was in places like this. That must be how people had escaped. But where would those stairs be?

I looked around for someone to ask but the last of the survivors, way too few, were already pushing their way out onto the street. I was left alone in the empty lobby.

To my left was a reception desk and on the wall behind it a building directory listing all the companies that rented here, and their suite numbers. I didn't see One World on that list. Were they hiding behind a false company name? It was what I would have done. Maybe it *was what I did*, I thought, *me being their erstwhile leader and all.*

There was no floor plan. But the fleeing people had come from somewhere and it must be the stairs. All I needed to do was follow their path in reverse.

I set off again, picking my way through the dimly lit lobby, and there, ahead of me on the far wall, I saw what I was looking for.

A door marked *Emergency Staircase.*

I picked up the pace, running the last several feet, and tugged at the door. When I opened it, there was a figure slumped on the other side.

It was Clara.

# CHAPTER FIFTEEN

FOR A MOMENT I thought she was dead, but then Clara looked up at me with a look of surprised relief.

"Hayden. Thank goodness you're here."

At first, I struggled to comprehend the situation. Clara was on her knees, bent over, which was what gave rise to my initial impression that she had collapsed in the stairwell and died. But now I saw another figure. A young woman with a nasty gash on her forehead. She was sitting with her back against the wall.

"What's going on?" I asked, all too aware that we were far from safe in the damaged building. "We have to leave, right now."

"That's what I was doing when I came across this woman." Clara stood up. "She collapsed before we could make it out. I couldn't leave her here."

"I'm fine now," the woman said, looking up at us. She tried to rise, grimaced, sank back down again. "Or maybe not."

"She has a bad head injury," I said, assessing the situation. "Probably a concussion, too."

"My office roof collapsed on me." The woman clenched her jaw in pain.

"We can't stay here," I said. "We'll carry her out."

"Right." Clara nodded.

"You take one arm, and I'll take the other."

Together we lifted the woman. She put an arm around my shoulder, and her other arm around Clara's.

Together, all three of us made our way across the lobby. It was slow going, made all the worse by an ominous groaning sound coming from above. Were the beams that held up the building starting to fail under the intense heat of the fire raging above?

"I thought you were dead," I told Clara as we moved toward the entrance.

"No you didn't," Clara replied. "Not deep down. Otherwise, you wouldn't have rushed in here looking for me."

I realized she was right. A part of me had never accepted the possibility that Clara was killed in the explosion. Or was it blind hope in the face of overwhelming odds to the contrary? After all, Clara had been on her way to the very floors that exploded. That brought up another question. "You must have reached One World before the blast. How did you survive?"

"I never got anywhere near that far." Clara hitched the injured woman higher on her shoulder and staggered forward. "I was going to take the elevator all the way up, almost did, but then I had second thoughts. If there really were operatives sent by the senator waiting up there, they would expect us to use the elevator. They would be watching it. I decided to ride as far as the eighteenth floor and take the stairs for the last six. Less obvious."

"Well, thank God you did." That decision had saved her life.

"Tell me about it. I'd barely stepped out of the elevator and found the stairs when I heard the explosion. Of course, I didn't know what had happened at first, but then people started coming down from the floors above. Pretty soon there was smoke filling the stairwell, so I knew it must be bad."

"It's bad, alright," I said as we reached the shattered front of the building. On the street outside I could see emergency personnel—police and paramedics—combing through the debris and wrecked vehicles looking for survivors. "A blast took out several floors, including the floor where One World was located."

"A bomb?" Clara asked as we stepped out onto the street.

"More than likely." A pair of paramedics rushed over to us, and we handed off the injured woman.

I was aware of cops milling around. Lots of them.

Were they here to help the wounded, or were they looking for us? Common sense said the former, but I decided it was best not to find out.

"Let's go." I took Clara by the hand. "Keep your head down and don't make eye contact with anyone. Do your best to look like a shell-shocked survivor."

"Shouldn't be too hard," Clara said. "I pretty much am one."

"I should never have let you go into that building on your own." We hurried away from the building. The street looked like something out of a post-apocalyptic movie. I took in the scene now in greater detail than I had before. Small fires burned where large pieces of debris had landed. Several cars were now nothing but smoking wrecks. Cloying, acrid smoke filled the air. There were more bodies than the one I had noticed before. Lots of them. Some were still in their destroyed vehicles. I saw others crushed under parts of the building that had crashed down when the explosion happened. And then there was that red purse, still sitting among the rubble. No one had bothered to move it, and why would they when there was so much other carnage all around.

What I thought to be a portent of Clara's fate was nothing of the sort. It was so much worse. A chilling reminder that somewhere, perhaps high above us in the burning building, its owner was dead.

"Hey, you two!" A voice called out to us.

I saw a uniformed officer out of the corner of my eye. He was looking at us and pointing.

"Keep moving. Pretend you didn't hear," I told Clara.

"Stop where you are." The officer was coming toward us, walking at a brisk pace. I noticed the palm of his hand resting on the butt of a gun in a holster on his belt.

"What are we going to do?" Clara asked, breathless. "He's following us."

"Don't slow down, but don't run either. If we take off, he'll think we're up to something. And whatever you do, don't look back."

"What do you think he wants?" Clara asked.

"I don't know. He may want to check our ID." Which would be bad because we didn't have any. "They must surely be looking for whoever bombed the building."

"Or they might be looking for us."

"Possible." In either case, we couldn't engage the cop. I wondered if news of our escape from the warehouse in the Packing District had reached the senator. They would have gone back to check on the bodies after that creature did its work. I also wondered if she and her cronies were behind the blast that had destroyed One World, because I was sure the organization was the target. It was too much of a coincidence to be anything else.

"I'll warn you one more time. Stop." The gun was coming out now. This was no friendly chat to see if we were okay or ask who we were and why we were there.

"We're in trouble," I said, hoping to see a way out of the situation. I braced myself for what might happen next. Would he shoot? But he didn't. Instead, I heard a thundering crash.

I risked a glance backward.

A long, sleek hyperloop train had whisked down the tracks

on its gantry above the street, oblivious to the carnage that lay ahead. When it reached the section of gantry destroyed by falling debris, the train kept going even though there was nothing left to support it. Carriages flew off one by one, narrow silver projectiles full of passengers, and crashed into the street on top of those who had escaped the building, and the emergency personnel who were trying to help them. People fled in all directions—the lucky ones who hadn't ended up crushed under the derailed carriages.

The cop had stopped his pursuit of us and turned to gaze at the unfolding nightmare in slack-jawed horror.

This was our chance. I looked around for an escape route and saw something better. A man hurrying toward us. Someone I recognized. It was Brooks. Somehow, someway, he was alive.

# CHAPTER SIXTEEN

"QUICKLY. COME WITH ME." Brooks reached us and motioned toward an alleyway between two buildings.

"What? No." Clara shook her head. "We can't leave those people back there. We have to go back and help them."

"Not going to happen," Brooks said. "*What we have to do* is get off the streets right away. It's not safe for you here."

"But the train . . . There must be so many injured people…"

"Not our problem."

"How can you say that?" Clara looked horrified.

"Easy," Brooks shot back, then sighed when he saw Clara's reaction. "Look, even if we did go back, what good would it do? There are paramedics on the scene already. Cops. Fire-fighters. Professionals who can help those people way better than we can."

"He's right," I said. "You saw that cop. He was coming after us. Something wasn't right. We go back there all we'll end up doing is getting ourselves arrested."

"And if that happens, you won't survive long enough to make bail," Brooks said. "You'll be taken somewhere off the grid and disappeared."

"Disappeared?"

"Murdered by the same people that tried to kill us in the Packing District." Brooks took her arm and moved off. "Now, come on."

Much to my relief, Clara followed him. "Did anyone else make it out of the warehouse," I asked.

"Only Colt so far as I know. We ran into each other outside the warehouse after the attack. The senator's people shot and killed Dansk, but Colt was wearing body armor under his shirt. It bought him enough time to run."

That was something at least, but it meant that five men had lost their lives. Three of those who accompanied us to the warehouse, and the two gunmen brooks had placed on the gantries as insurance. "How did you find us."

"Luck. We were on our way back to headquarters when the explosion happened." He glanced back at the destroyed skyscraper. "Bastards."

"Who did this?" Clara asked.

"Who do you think?" there was anger in Brooks' voice.

The question didn't require an answer. We all knew the likely culprits. The senator and whoever was pulling her strings.

"Where are we going?" I asked as we reached the alleyway.

"Somewhere safe," Brooks replied as he led us off the street.

I glanced back over my shoulder as we stepped into the alley. The street was a fiery mess. The cop must have forgotten about us, at least temporarily. He was still transfixed by the horrific scene in front of him.

"Where is Colt?" I asked.

"Not far."

We traversed the alley, crossed another street. Entered an enclosed courtyard at the base of a gleaming spire that lanced skyward like a colossal needle. Brooks ushered us to the back of this open space, near a bronze statue of a man I didn't recognize.

"What are we doing here?" Clara asked.

"Regrouping," replied Brooks.

Colt stepped out from behind the statue. He looked relieved to see us. The feeling was mutual.

"Glad you're both alive," he said.

"Not as much as we are." I ran a hand through my hair to dislodge the dust that had settled there. "What now?"

"Colt will take you somewhere to lay low," Brooks said. "A place only a few trusted members of our organization know about."

"You mean a safe house."

"If you want to call it that."

"This is insane." Clara looked like she was about to lose it. "First, they set a monster loose on us, then a bomb goes off and destroys an entire building. There must be hundreds of people dead. What kind of a world is this?"

"The kind where powerful people, rich people, don't want the status quo rocked by folk like Hayden."

"But how can they get away with such a thing?"

"You're assuming the public will ever even know the true perpetrators. Don't forget, the same people who blew up that building also control the media."

"Not to mention the police, judiciary, prison system," said Colt. "Which is why this conversation can wait until later."

Brooks nodded in agreement. "The senator and her colleagues will have checked the warehouse by now and discovered there are less bodies than there should be, I'm sure. Our faces will be on every wanted list within hours."

"Might already be," Colt said. "You can guess who they will blame for that explosion."

"Yeah." Brooks rubbed his chin. "All the more reason to lay low."

Colt nodded. "All right then, let's get moving."

"What about you?" I asked, turning to Brooks.

"I'll be along later. I need to find out if anyone else survived first."

"That's a terrible idea." Colt glared at him. "You saw that explosion. There's no way anyone on the twenty-fourth floor could have survived."

"I have to try. I found Hayden and Clara, didn't I?"

"Only because we hadn't made it up there yet," I said. Our narrow escape was only now sinking in. "And you said it yourself, we need to get away from here, not go back."

"Besides, Colt's right," Clara said. "No one up there could have survived. I should know. I was in the building when it blew."

"Which means Kellerman is dead," Colt said to Brooks. "You're in charge now. Next in line. Except for Hayden that is, and until we get his memories back, he's pretty much useless." Colt looked at me. "No offence."

"None taken." I wasn't sure I wanted to lead these people.

"You're right. I am in charge," Brooks said. "Which means I get to decide what happens. And right now, I'm ordering you to take Hayden and Clara to the safe house. I'm going to have a look around, make sure we're not leaving anyone behind. I'll join you there when I can."

Colt folded his arms and glared but didn't move.

Brooks narrowed his eyes. "You have a problem with that?"

"No, sir." Colt's answer was curt. His tone contradicted his words.

"Good. Now get them out of here."

"For the record, I think you're making a bad decision." Colt stepped out from the shadow of the statue. He looked back at us. "Don't just stand there, let's go."

# CHAPTER SEVENTEEN

"How are we going to rescue Darwin now?" Clara asked.

We were in the safe house, which was in reality a small apartment in one of the drab concrete monstrosities we had passed as we walked through the slum situated beyond the river from downtown.

I stood at the window and gazed out toward the skyscrapers that dominated the heart of the city. From this vantage point, I couldn't see what was left of the building that contained One World's headquarters—there were too many other high-rises in the way—but the column of smoke that rose into the evening sky pinpointed its location well enough.

I pulled my gaze away and turned to look at Clara, who was sitting on a ratty couch with her hands placed neatly in her lap. She looked back at me, hoping for an answer I couldn't give. Instead, I told her the truth. "I don't think we can unless there's another machine somewhere that can punch between realities."

"There's not," Colt said. He was leaning against the wall near the door with his arms folded and a stony expression on his face. "Outside of a government facility, at least."

"Then that's where we should go."

"Right. Because they're going to let us waltz in there and then look the other way while we reset their machines to the coordinates of that collapsing world, hop across and get him, then watch us stroll back out like nothing happened." Colt was pulling no punches. His boss hadn't yet reappeared, and he was in a foul mood. "But hey, it's a great idea if you want to end up dead."

"There's no need to be facetious." Clara wasn't ready to give up yet. "There must be another way. Someone else with the technology we need."

"There isn't, trust me," Colt said. "You don't want to know how hard it was to get our hands on the technology we used to rescue you. Had to build half of it from scratch and steal the parts for the rest."

"It's hopeless, then."

"Pretty much."

"This day keeps getting worse." Clara sat back and folded her arms. She was still wearing the clothes she had on when we left to meet the senator earlier that day, but the soot and grime were gone now at least. We had both taken a much-needed shower at the first opportunity. Colt had promised us fresh clothes, too, but that would take some time.

"If you build a machine to move between realities once, what's stopping you from doing it again?" I asked.

"Resources for a start," Colt replied. "The components are not easy to come by. And even if we could assemble everything we need, there's the little problem of knowing how to put it together. It's not like you can download schematics from the internet."

There was internet in this world. That was something familiar to cling to, at least. "You've already done it once."

"Which means you already have the schematics." Clara took up the reins, voicing what I was thinking.

"If only it were that easy." Colt sounded glum. "It took six months to build the last one and another three to ensure it was safe before we used it. Even then, we had some hiccups."

"Like what?" I asked.

"Like trying to cross over twice in a short time period and killing an entire team."

"Which is why we couldn't go straight back and get Darwin in the first place," I said.

"Correct."

"Hardly what I'd call a little hiccup. Is that the five men Kellerman told us about last night?"

"Yes. One of them was your best friend and right-hand man." Colt hesitated for a few seconds before speaking again, gauging my reaction. "John Bradley."

If he was expecting a shocked reaction from me, he didn't get it. The name meant nothing. I didn't remember a John Bradley any more than I remembered Kellerman or Brooks. Of course, Kellerman was probably dead now, too.

I did some mental arithmetic in my head. "If it took you that long to build the machine, it means…"

"You hadn't been sent over yet. You were the one who came up with the idea to build it in the first place. Kind of funny, really. If it wasn't for your crazy scheme—which no one thought would work, by the way—we wouldn't have been able to go in and rescue you."

"If it was so hard to do, how *did you* get it to work?"

"We had a little help there. That was also thanks to you. One of the scientists who worked on the original government project. You not only convinced her to share the schematics, but also to help us build the machine."

"And how did I do that?"

"You never told us how. All I know is that you turned her into a believer for the cause. Maybe when you get your memories back, you'll find out how."

"If I ever get my memories back." I wasn't going to hold my breath on that one. So far, despite being bombarded with the people and places of my alleged past, I had not regained a single recollection that I could attribute to anything other than the life I remembered. The life where I was an author living in Vermont.

"If this woman shared the knowledge of how to build the machine with you, why can't you build another one?" Clara asked.

It was the question I was about to ask as well.

"Because everything was inside her head. Professor Morecambe had an incredible mind. She forgot nothing, even if she'd only seen it for a split second."

"An eidetic memory," I said.

"Yes. Although she kept that particular skill from her colleagues. When you're working in a top-secret lab for a shady government agency performing experiments that you probably shouldn't, total recall is not an asset. It's hard to keep something secret when classified documents can be carried out stored inside the head of the researcher who looked at them."

"Especially if those classified documents are blueprints for technology that can open a wormhole between realities."

"Exactly."

"That still doesn't answer my question," Clara said. "Why can't we ask her to build a new one?"

Colt cleared his throat. "Because she's dead."

# CHAPTER EIGHTEEN

BROOKS ARRIVED at the safe house an hour after it got dark outside. He looked tired, worn down. When he stepped into the apartment, his shoulders visibly slumped.

Colt shot him a questioning look but didn't ask.

Brooks replied anyway. "No one left."

Colt nodded slowly.

"I looked for as long as I dared. There are police everywhere. The safe house isn't going to be safe for long." He looked at Clara and me. "You'll have to leave the city. Sooner rather than later."

"Why the rush?" I asked.

As an answer, Brooks picked up the remote control for a paper-thin flatscreen TV mounted on the wall and clicked it on. He found a news channel.

On the screen was a picture of the burning building and the devastated street below. A perky female newscaster with perfect auburn hair and sparkling green eyes was framed in a box superimposed over the horrific scene in the bottom left corner. She was clearly on location, but at least a couple of blocks from the epicenter of the disaster, probably stuck behind a press cordon set up by the police. Her mouth moved silently as a chyron scrolled across the bottom of the screen, relaying short bursts of information about the explosion and its aftermath.

Brooks turned up the volume.

The woman's voice filled the room. She was talking to someone off-camera. A studio presenter maybe. "That's right Alton. The city's anti-terrorism unit has been on the scene for almost four hours now, and I can tell you, they're taking this very seriously."

The view shifted to the studio, and there was the other presenter. A man in his late thirties with a square jaw and glasses that made him look almost austere. Serious. The on-site presenter was relegated to a quarter of the screen.

The male presenter, presumably this was Alton, nodded gravely. "Thanks, Melody. That ties in with the information that has been coming out of police headquarters. This is indeed a terrorist attack and not some unfortunate accident."

Melody's wavy hair fluttered in the breeze. Her perfect makeup, ruby-red lips, and carefully selected wardrobe stood in stark contrast to the chaotic scene upon which she was reporting. "I don't see how it could be anything else, Alton. The scope of the devastation, the location of the explosion, bears all the hallmarks of a terrorist group."

Alton, sitting behind a desk in the studio, was still nodding as if this made him appear more serious. "And as we learned a short while ago, the police have received a communication already claiming responsibility for this horrendous act."

"Indeed," Melody agreed. "A dissident group that goes by the name One World."

I looked at Brooks. "What the hell?"

Brooks said nothing. He merely pointed to draw my attention back to the screen.

Melody wasn't done. "According to the authorities, the group rented a suite in this building on the twenty-fourth floor several months ago. The speculation right now is that they used this suite to set up their bomb, and then detonated it when the street below was at its busiest."

Alton's head was still moving slowly up and down. He reminded me of one of those novelty nodding dogs that people used to put in their cars. "Timed to create maximum casualties."

"It certainly created casualties, Alton. Lots of them. At this moment, the death toll stands at a hundred and forty-six, with over two hundred injured. Some of those are in critical condition. Not to mention the destruction to property. Of course, those numbers are fluid and changing as more information comes in. There could be many more people trapped on the higher floors of the building."

"Many more casualties," Alton said.

"Undoubtedly. The people who did this need to be taken off the streets, and fast."

"Which is why the police have released information about this group so quickly," Alton said in the studio. The graphic behind him changed from the devastation and burning building to a grainy photograph of the street with a date stamp that matched the moments after the explosion. "This still image was pulled from a surveillance camera two blocks from the scene."

At first, I didn't understand the significance of the image, but then I saw two figures hurrying away from the skyscraper at about the moment the cop challenged us. It was me and Clara.

Alton was still speaking as the image zoomed in to show us in better detail. I was relieved to see that our faces were lost to the grainy video. "The police believe these are the pair who triggered the bomb. Right now, they haven't been positively identified, but they will, Melody. And fast."

"They need to," replied the perky presenter. "Because I'm sensing a palpable fear on the streets down here, Alton. People are wondering if there are more bombs, and I don't blame them."

"That's why the authorities have closed off downtown, melody. They're making a sweep of the other buildings as we speak, looking for—"

Brooks turned the TV off, silencing the presenters.

I stared at the empty screen in disbelief. "How are they blaming One World for this?"

"Why wouldn't they?" Brooks replied. "What better way to silence your critics than to make them the enemy? Turn people against them."

"But a bomb?" Clara looked up at us. "Killing all those people simply to make you out as the bad guys?"

"It's been done before," I said. "The Reichstag in 1933. Germany's parliament building before it burned to the ground. The Nazis blamed Communists and used the fire to roll back constitutional protections that allowed the Nazi party to take control. They suspended freedom of the press, right of assembly, and gave the police broad powers they hadn't previously possessed."

"But it wasn't communists."

"No. The Nazi party orchestrated the fire themselves."

"A self-inflicted wound to blame their enemy," Clara said.

"That's exactly what it was."

"Except you're quoting the history of an artificially created world and drawing on implanted memories."

"Actually, he's not." Brooks stepped forward. "The alternate realities use real history as their backdrop. The false memories you were given contain the history of our own, real world. At least until the early twenty-first century."

"Because that's the time period re-created in these false realities," Clara said.

"That's right." Brooks replied. "In the real world, everything went downhill fast after that. No one wanted to re-create the troubles of the past hundred and fifty years. The runaway global warming and overpopulation. The global wars over resources that almost destroyed us."

"And yet the people who really planted that bomb have learned nothing."

"History always repeats itself," I said. I looked at Brooks. "Don't you think it's strange that they didn't mention any of us by name in that news report? After all, they were quick to assign blame to One World. They even went as far as saying the organization has claimed responsibility."

"It's not strange," Brooks replied. "Think about it. We were supposed to have died in that warehouse. The bomb was timed to go off a short time later. First, they kill us, then they discredit our organization."

"With the leadership gone and the rest of One World either killed in the explosion or on the run, there would be no one left to cry foul."

"Public opinion would turn against us." Brooks walked to the window and looked out. "Crackpot terrorists."

"That might change once they realize we escaped the warehouse," Colt said.

"My thoughts exactly." Brooks turned back to us. "Our mugshots will be on every news channel across the country once they realize it's the only way to locate us."

"Who cares," Clara said. "Regardless of what the government says, we didn't bomb that building. People will listen to Hayden Stone. At least if what you've told us is correct. We'll tell the truth. After all, he returned from an alternate reality."

"You're being naïve," Brooks told her. "These people are smart. All the evidence would point back to Hayden Stone and One World. No one will believe a word any of us say."

"But—"

Brooks cut Clara off. "And anyway, what makes you think we'll even get the chance to tell our side of things? These are powerful people with a lot to lose. They will be ruthless in dealing with us."

"That's it, then." I couldn't see a way out of this situation. It didn't matter where we went, how far we ran. We were up against impossible odds. "We're done for."

Brooks shook his head. "Not necessarily. Don't you still want to find Darwin?"

"You know we do," I replied. "But the machine that would allow us to do so was in a building that blew up. It's gone. Destroyed."

"Then we build another one. You get Darwin back, and we get proof of those collapsing worlds to save our hides."

"And how are we going to do that, exactly?" I asked.

Brooks remained silent for a moment, as if he was gauging whether he should say anything more. Then he sighed. "We go to the person who helped us build it in the first place. Professor Belinda Morecambe."

I shot Colt a questioning look. "You said she was dead."

Brooks stepped in before Colt could say anything. "She is dead as far as the world outside this room is concerned. It was the only way to ensure her safety. But Belinda Morecambe is very much alive and kicking."

# CHAPTER NINETEEN

"Professor Morecambe is still alive?" The look of surprise on Colt's face told me he had no clue that the woman who helped One World build a machine to open a wormhole between dimensions was still alive. He fell silent for a moment, absorbing this turn of events, before asking an obvious question. "How is that possible?"

"We faked her death in order to keep her safe," Brooks said. "She is currently living under an assumed identity."

"How many people know about this?" Colt asked.

"Not many. Kellerman. A few other people at the top of the organization."

"You didn't share this with the rest of us?" Colt sounded annoyed. His gaze shifted to me. "Did he know?"

"I don't know anything worth a damn since they apparently wiped my memory," I said. "I don't even remember you guys before yesterday, let alone this professor."

"Hayden knew about it," Brooks said in a calm voice. "It was his idea to give her a new identity before the authorities found out what she'd done."

"Because if that happened, they would have killed her," Clara said.

"Without a doubt." Brooks nodded. "She trusted Hayden the most. That was probably the only reason she went along with the scheme."

"How did you…" Hayden paused and rephrased his question. "How did *we* fake her death?"

"Car accident. Her vehicle went off the Beckett Williams Downtown Bridge during a storm and into the water. They never found a body, of course, but we left enough cloned material in the vehicle, along with some of her own blood, to make it convincing. There would be no reason for the authorities to think it was anything other than a tragic mishap."

"And no one ever suspected she was working with One World?" I asked.

Brooks shook his head. "Not so far as we knew. And you wanted to keep it that way. Keep her safe."

"What happened to her?" I plunged deep into the depths of my mind for any morsel of information that might have survived regarding the events that Brooks was describing but came up empty. It was a weird sensation to discuss things I had done but could not recall. I was a stranger standing on the outside of my own life. "Where did she go after the accident?"

"Not far. She stayed in the city under a false identity, for a while at least. We kept her at arms-length. Didn't allow her to interact with anyone outside of a few people at One World who knew the truth. You said that was important. The less people who were aware she was still alive, the safer she would be."

"That makes sense." It sounded like something I would say. "Where is she now?"

"Therein lies the problem." Brooks looked uncomfortable. "After you got captured and sent into that alternate universe, she became obsessed with finding you. She wanted us to do more. She harassed Kellerman at every opportunity to send more teams to look for you on the other side. He was cautious, knew that too many jumps would draw attention. The machine used a lot of power. Much more than the norm for a downtown office building. That was one concern. But there was another issue. The technology left a telltale signature every time it punched between dimensions. A neutrino trail. Kellerman was worried that if the authorities detected it, we would be discovered. Belinda Morecambe—although that wasn't her name now, of course—disagreed with him. She thought it was worth the risk. It caused an argument, and she left."

"If she was so desperate to find Hayden," Clara asked, "why would she leave?"

"You'll have to ask her that if and when you find her."

"You still haven't answered my question," I said.

"That's because I'm not entirely sure. After her disagreement with Kellerman, she went to ground. Left the city."

"And she never told anyone where she was going?"

"No. She was pretty angry. The only person she would still speak to was me. Probably because I was more on her side than Kellerman and the few others who knew she was still alive. I tried to find out where she was going, but she wouldn't say. All she would tell me was that you and she had made plans for an eventuality where she would have to leave the city. She said there were arrangements in place."

"Arrangements?" I asked. "What kind of arrangements?"

Brooks shrugged. "She wouldn't say."

"Well, this is ripe," Colt said. "The only person who could tell us where Professor Morecambe went doesn't even remember her."

"That isn't exactly true," Brooks said. "She left a message with me, should we ever locate you. Said it would allow you to find her."

"Then you do know where she is." I wondered if Brooks was playing games. He was talking in circles.

"No, I really don't." Brooks reached into his pocket and

pulled out what looked like a silver credit card. It was blank except for a tiny dot-like lens at the top, mounted flush with the surface. It looked almost printed, but I could see light reflecting off the lens glass. He held the card out to me. "She gave me this. Said she had recorded a message in case we ever found you."

"What's on it?" I asked.

"I couldn't say." Brooks pressed the object into my palm. "It's encrypted. High-level stuff. Almost impossible to hack. Only a combination of your face and touch DNA can unlock the message."

"Maybe she's telling you where to find her," Clara said hopefully.

"That would be my guess," said Brooks. "And let's hope I'm right, because the only way that you will get Darwin back, or that we will be able to get proof of the collapsing universes and clear our names, is if she wants you to find her."

"How do I use this thing?" I asked, turning the card over in my hand.

"Hold the card in front of your face, with the lens pointing toward you."

I did as I was told.

"That's it," Brooks said. "Now give it a moment to recognize you."

I saw the lens shift. A barely perceptible movement.

A smooth female voice from nowhere said, "Identity confirmed. Card access granted."

"Okay, it worked." Brooks rubbed his hands together. "Now we're getting somewhere."

"What happens next?" I asked. The card had done nothing else, although I wasn't sure what I expected it to do.

"Just watch," Brooks said. "Give it a moment."

I watched.

Clara stepped close and peered over my shoulder.

The others gathered around, all eyes on the smooth silver card.

For a second, nothing happened, then the surface changed, brightened.

Three words appeared.

*Come to Fahrenheit.*

# CHAPTER TWENTY

"COME TO FAHRENHEIT?" I read the message aloud. "What the hell does that mean?"

Colt and Brooks exchanged a glance.

"What? Am I missing something?"

"If she went to Fahrenheit, we've got a hell of a trip ahead of us."

"Would someone please tell me what Fahrenheit is?" I was getting tired of missing the joke. Not that I had found anything funny since the gas station in Vermont.

"It's an outpost on the California border up by Lake Tahoe. Used to be known as Stateline back in the day. It's one of the few settlements left on the west coast after the quake of eighty-six drove away most of the remaining population. Took a pretty bad beating. Most of the original buildings were destroyed but some of the residents refused to leave."

"God knows why," Colt said. "The lake lost half its water overnight during the quake, destroying most of the fresh water in the area. That, coupled with losses from the drought ravaging the area, reduced the lake to little more than a puddle."

"And without fresh water, it's hard to survive," Brooks said. "Fahrenheit is pretty much a lawless frontier town these days. Not a place I want to visit."

"Not to mention, we'll have to travel through the Arizona Cauldron to get there." Colt didn't look happy. "That's going to be fun."

"Arizona Cauldron?" I had done nothing but play perpetual catch-up ever since my feet landed on the soil of this world.

"A huge swath of land that encompasses a large section of the West, including Arizona, New Mexico, Colorado, Utah, and sections of Nevada. It's practically uninhabitable, along with most of the western seaboard, thanks to natural disasters, extreme heat, and drought."

"Not a fun place to be," Colt said. "Hundreds of miles of arid landscape with very few pockets of humanity left."

"Can't we fly over it?" Clara asked.

"Not if we want to avoid getting caught," said Brooks. "Too many ways to get spotted at an airport. Facial recognition. Biometrics. No-fly list. You name it."

Colt agreed with him. "We'd never make it past the gate."

"And anyway, even if we could avoid detection, flying isn't an option. There are barely any airlines that go out West anymore. Most of the airports are gone, either destroyed in the quake of eighty-six or bankrupt."

"So how are we going to get there?" Clara asked.

"A good old-fashioned road trip."

"You mean we drive?"

"Better than walking," Brooks said.

Clara looked unsure. "How long will that take?"

"Several days, maybe a week. Depends on what we run into along the way."

"And if we can get out of the city without being noticed," Colt said. "We're public enemy number one right now."

"All the more reason to leave quickly." Brooks looked toward Colt. "We'll need supplies. Fresh clothes. Provisions."

"And a vehicle," Colt added. He glanced toward the door. "I have contacts. I can get everything we need by morning."

Brooks nodded. "Make it happen."

Colt's attention shifted to me and Clara. "I'll need your measurements if I'm going to get clothes that fit you."

"I'm a size six," said Clara. "Don't forget the less obvious stuff."

"I'll do my best," said Colt. His gaze dropped to her chest. "I need to know . . . well . . . "

"34D," Clara told him, a slight blush coming to her cheeks.

Colt nodded, then looked at me.

I told him my measurements.

"That's all I need." Colt took a step toward the door. "I'm going to make the arrangements. I'll be back soon."

"Is it still safe here?" Clara asked after Colt had left. "He could get caught and bring the authorities."

"He won't get caught," Brooks said, reassuring her. "And even if he did, Colt wouldn't talk. I trust him with my life."

"You're trusting him with our lives, too," I said. Maybe if my original memories were intact, I would have agreed with Brooks, but they weren't. The last twenty-four hours had been a whirlwind of steadily worsening situations. Now we were expected to sit in the safe house and hope that the man who was arranging transportation and supplies to get us out of the city returned safely.

"It's not worth worrying about," Brooks said. "There isn't anywhere better for us to go. If the authorities come looking for us here, if they somehow discover our safe house, then we'll fight until we can fight no longer. But if you're unsure about Colt, you needn't be. I'm vouching for him."

"Fair enough." I shrugged. I was still holding the card in

my hand. Now I looked down at it again, and the message had changed.

*Bring this with you.*

*Don't lose it.*

*Come quickly and stay safe.*

I held it up for the others to see. "Look."

Brooks eyed the new message. "I guess we have our marching orders."

Clara leaned in closer. "Are we sure we can trust this?"

"What do you mean?" Brooks asked.

"That message could be from anyone. We could walk into another trap like we did the warehouse."

"Not likely." Brooks shook his head. "The messages are all prerecorded. Belinda wouldn't risk a direct connection to the web."

"This device can do that?" I asked, incredulous. It was so small and thin, not even as big as a credit card. "Connect to the internet?"

"It can do a lot of things. Think of it like a cross between a cell phone and a laptop computer in your world, only shrunk down many times."

"How could you use that as a laptop?" Clara asked, looking bewildered.

"I didn't say it *was* a laptop. It can do a lot of things a 21st-century laptop could not, but you don't use it the same way."

"If it can access the web, it can be manipulated," I said.

"Not this one. The security protocols programmed into it will be too strong and its digital footprint will be anonymous. Professor Morecambe would have made sure of that."

"What about if someone got hold of the card itself?" I asked. "Could they hack it then?"

"No. And anyway, she gave me the card in person. I've had it in my possession ever since. No one has tampered with the card and it's not a trap."

"I hope you're right," I said.

"So do I." Brooks walked back to the window and gazed out over the skyline and the thick plume of smoke still rising over downtown. "Because we have nowhere else to go."

# CHAPTER TWENTY-ONE

COLT DIDN'T RETURN until four hours later. When he did arrive back at the safe house, he looked worn out.

He carried a large duffel bag, which he put on the table. "There's a change of clothes for each of us in here. Toiletries and food, too."

My heart leaped when I heard that. None of us had eaten all day. I was starving, and I knew the others were as well.

Brooks unzipped the bag and emptied the contents onto the table. As promised, there were fresh clothes for each of us, toothbrushes, toothpaste, and deodorant.

Among the food items brought back by Colt were bread, milk, deli meat, and cheese. There was also coffee and an assortment of snacks, like chips and chocolate.

Clara slipped into mother mode and went about preparing a quick and easy meal for us.

While she did so, I turned my attention to Colt. "Did you find a vehicle?"

Colt nodded. "It's hardly a luxury ride, but it will get us where we need to go. I parked in the garage under the building. There are more provisions in the trunk, including water, food that won't spoil, clothing, and a few other items that might come in useful."

I didn't press him on what the other items might be. Instead, I looked at Brooks. "We shouldn't stay here any longer than necessary."

"I agree." Brooks was watching Clara prepare the food. He was hungry, too. "But not yet. We are all exhausted. I suggest that we eat, then get some sleep before setting off. We'll leave an hour before dawn."

"That should give us enough time to get out of the city before the sun comes up," said Colt.

"What if they're looking for us already?" I asked. "We will be easier to spot if the roads are empty."

"Oh, they will be looking for us," Brooks said. "You can mark my words on that."

"But the roads are never empty." Colt went to the window and drew the blinds, then turned back to us. "Night or day, there's always traffic. Darkness will make it harder for the street cams to identify us."

"We have to worry about cameras?" I groaned inwardly. Everything about this world was hard.

"There's surveillance everywhere downtown. I can't believe you only showed up on one camera earlier when you were fleeing the explosion. Thank heavens the police couldn't identify your faces."

"Unless they did and are keeping it under wraps," Colt said.

"Either way, it doesn't matter." Brooks shrugged. "We can't control that stuff. What we *can do* is make the best choices available and hope our luck holds."

"We leave before dawn, then." I glanced sideways at Clara. She was finishing up preparing four plates of sandwiches.

If she had an opinion, she didn't voice it. Instead, she

looked up with a slight smile on her face. The first I'd seen since we landed in this strange and dangerous world.

"Foods up, boys," she said, bringing the plates loaded with sandwiches to the table. And then we ate.

# CHAPTER TWENTY-TWO

THE SAFE HOUSE had two small bedrooms. I occupied one, along with Clara, while Brooks and Colt took turns to share the other because we had decided that someone should remain awake at all times and keep guard. I volunteered to split shifts with them, but Brooks declined, saying that my lack of memory was a liability and that I might not recognize a threat until it was too late. I was too tired to bother arguing.

It was a little after midnight now, and I lay in bed with Clara's head resting on my shoulder and my arm around her. I thought she would fall asleep as soon as she crawled into bed, but she didn't.

"What do you think Darwin is doing right now?" She asked, looking up at me with wide eyes.

"I don't know." I couldn't see the point in idle speculation.

"Do you think he's dead?"

"I think he's fine," I lied. The last time I had seen Darwin, we were trapped in the lobby of an office building with crazies clamoring at the doors. They had given us bracelets—technology that allowed us to move between realities—and now we were here.

Darwin was not.

His bracelet had malfunctioned. The last thing I saw before the world I knew evaporated and I found myself here, were the lobby doors slamming back and crazies pouring in toward us . . . toward Darwin.

It was impossible to know if he had escaped that lobby-and I certainly hoped that he had-but the longer we waited, the less chance we had that he was still alive. This had weighed heavily on me all day. Over twenty-four hours had passed since our rescue and now the machine that made it possible was gone. Destroyed by the same people who tried to kill us in the warehouse. Our only hope was a woman I didn't even remember, who was an entire country distant from us.

"How will he survive long enough for us to find that professor?" Clara asked, giving voice to the same question that rattled through my mind.

This time, I was truthful. "I don't know."

"What if she can't help us rebuild the machine?"

My answer was the same. "I don't know."

Clara lapsed into silence for a minute or two, lost in thought. Then she spoke again. "Do you think we can trust Brooks and Colt? I mean, really trust them to get us all the way across the country. Because our lives will depend upon it."

"I—"

"If you're going to answer with 'I don't know' for a fourth time, rethink it."

"How do you want me to answer?"

"Try telling me that everything's going to be okay. That Brooks and Colt know what they're doing and won't get us killed. That we'll be able to prove our innocence before we end up tried as terrorists or shot on the spot. How about you say that Darwin is fine and we'll rebuild the machine and rescue him."

"That's what you want me to say?"

"Yes."

"Even though it might not be the truth?"

"Yes."

"Ok." I stroked Clara's hair as my hand roamed down her back. My fingers grazed her cool bare skin. Her body pressed against me, warm and soft. I told her what she wanted to hear. All of it. And then we fell asleep in each other's arms.

# CHAPTER TWENTY-THREE

CLARA'S SCREAM pulled me from sleep with a jolt.

I opened my eyes and saw her sitting upright in the bed, a pale white form in the darkness with the covers crumpled around her waist. She was staring off into the corner of the room.

"What's wrong?" I pushed myself up and followed her gaze but saw nothing.

"You didn't see it?" Her voice trembled.

"See what?" The room looked as it had when we climbed into bed. Small, drab, sparsely furnished. The clothes that Cole had acquired for us sat folded on a wooden chair near the opposite wall. The clothes we had been wearing when we crossed over to this world lay in a pile on the floor.

"There's something here."

"What?" I still saw nothing. "What did you see?"

Before she could answer me, the bedroom door burst open, and Brooks rushed in. "Everything all right in here?"

Clara grabbed at the sheets to cover herself, holding them against her chest. "No. It's not."

"She had a bad dream, that's all," I said to Brooks.

"I didn't have a bad dream." Clara glared at me.

"Then what was it?" I could see Colt lingering in the doorway behind Brooks. His eyes were bleary, and he rubbed them. He must have been sleeping when Clara screamed.

"A crazy." Clara's attention was still fixed on the corner of the room opposite the bed. "There was a crazy in here with us. Watching us."

"That's impossible." There was no one but the four of us in the room. No crazies. No monsters.

"I know what I saw." Clara's voice lifted in anger. "It was a crazy."

"A crazy?" Brooks echoed. "You mean those half-human monstrosities that infest the reality we found you in?"

"Yes." Clara pointed toward the corner of the room. "I woke up, and it was standing right over there looking at me."

Brooks crossed the room. "Well, it's not here now."

"Maybe you were having a nightmare and hadn't fully woken up." I said to her. "Could it have been a fragment of your dream?"

"No, I don't, it was . . . well . . . I don't know." Clara sounded unsure of herself. She looked at me. "Maybe. I mean, I didn't see it for very long."

"All right, then. I'm going back to bed." Colt retreated from the doorway. I heard his footsteps as he crossed the small living room dining combination and then a door closed.

"We all good here?" Brooks asked.

"Yes. Thank you," Clara said sheepishly.

I watched him head for the door. "I guess it was a false alarm."

"Apparently." Brooks paused in the doorway. "Get some sleep. We'll be moving out in a couple of hours."

"Everything okay out there?" I asked him. "No sign of the cops or anyone else?"

"You think I'd be here standing calm as can be if there was?" Brooks reached for the door handle. "See you in a few hours."

When he was gone, Clara collapsed back onto the bed. "That was embarrassing."

"You had a bad dream, that's all. Could happen to any of us." I settled down beside her.

"I screamed like I was being murdered and there wasn't even anything there." Clara made an annoyed huffing sound in the darkness. "Those two men must think I'm a lunatic."

"I'm sure they have bigger things on their minds," I assured her.

"You really think it was a dream?"

"What else could it be?" I knew Clara thought she saw something, but I had seen nothing out of place. The room was empty. No crazies. That was all there was to it. I wasn't even sure how a crazy could have even gotten into a bedroom a whole universe away from where they existed.

"It was so real." Clara nestled against me. Her hand rested on my shoulder. "I swear, I saw it plain as day."

"I believe you."

"And then it was gone."

"Because it was a fragment of your dream. That's all." I held her tight. Kissed the top of her head. "You've been through a lot in the last week. It's no wonder you're having nightmares."

"And hallucinating, apparently."

"Hypnagogia."

"What?"

"That's what it's called. Hypnagogia. A transitional state between wakefulness and sleep, where the two mingle and you see elements of your dream in the real world."

"How on earth do you know that?" Clara pushed herself up and looked at me.

"I'm an author." As I spoke the words I realized they weren't actually true. I wasn't an author. That was the false life I'd been given to allow me to accept my new reality in an alternate universe.

Clara slid back down again under the covers. "And I'm a gas station attendant. What does that have to do with anything?"

"Research," I explained. "One of the characters in a book I wrote years ago suffered from waking dreams."

"I thought you were getting your first book published right before we met." Clara said. "You were going to New York for a celebration with your brother."

"I said it was a book I wrote, not one that got published. It's still sitting on the hard drive of the laptop I used to write on, back in Vermont..." I hesitated, realizing again that none of it had been real. "Back in the alternate reality Vermont."

"I'd love to read it one day."

"Why? It's part of the backstory they gave me. I didn't actually write it."

"I'd still like to read it. And the one you were getting published."

"It wasn't published yet. I got a book deal, but that was about as far as it had gone."

"Tell me what it was about," Clara said. "The book you were getting published. Tell me that story."

"I don't think we have time to read an entire book," I said with a smile.

"I don't mean read it to me. I know you can't do that. You don't even have the manuscript here. Tell me what it was about. Give me the short version."

"Sure. Why not?" I could tell we weren't going to get any more sleep. Clara was too nervous, and I was too awake. So I rubbed her back and told her the story of my book.

# CHAPTER TWENTY-FOUR

WE LEFT in the pre-dawn darkness. Brooks drove while Colt took shotgun. I sat with Clara in the back.

The car was like nothing we had ever ridden in before. There was no engine noise or vibration. It glided smoothly along as if riding a cushion of air. The cockpit comprised nothing but an X-shaped steering wheel and a dash that appeared to be made out of the same material as the credit card-sized device Professor Morecambe had given Brooks to pass on to me should I ever return to the real world. It glowed with information like our speed, direction, and a 3-D map displaying the road ahead of us. There were no knobs or buttons to be seen. No vents or grills, even though the climate inside the vehicle remained at a steady and comfortable temperature.

Brooks wasn't even really driving. He occupied the seat in front of the steering wheel—if you could call it that—but the car itself handled the driving after he fed it a destination. Everything was completely hands-off.

We had piled into the car a little before five in the morning. Colt had parked at the back of the garage in an inconspicuous location, even though it was unlikely anyone would notice the car or even care who it belonged to. Maybe he was worried about being spotted. That someone followed him back when he was out picking up the items necessary for our road trip. Or maybe he was naturally cautious. Either way it wasn't a problem, and we were soon riding through the narrow streets and out of the slum heading away from downtown. We passed through the Packing District, which took longer than I would have liked thanks to the ever-present glut of commercial traffic, and then as the first rays of morning sun stretched across the landscape, we entered another sprawling area of dilapidated housing that bore a striking resemblance to the shantytowns in places like Brazil, Mexico, and India.

These improvised dwellings, built with leftover and scavenged materials, hugged the road on each side. The narrow spaces between the buildings were teeming with bedraggled people that watched us pass by on the road, which was now pretty much free of traffic except for trucks barreling in the other direction as if they wanted to pass through this hellscape as quickly as possible.

A couple of times, people threw stones at the car, one of which hit the windshield and bounced off doing no damage.

It made Clara jump, though, and she let out a small squeal of alarm.

Colt twisted around to peer into the back. "Sorry about that. Hardly anyone ventures this far out of the city, at least on this road, for obvious reasons. There's not much out here except this place, and a lot of folk that live in Scraptown aren't exactly friendly."

"Scraptown? Really." Even the name was depressing.

"A fairly obvious moniker for a place like this I admit," Brooks said.

"If people avoid this area, then why are we passing through it?" I asked.

"Flying under the radar," Colt replied. "The interstate

runs about a dozen miles south of here. Ten lanes of smooth asphalt in each direction. It would be quicker, for sure, but it's also equipped with sophisticated surveillance systems to monitor traffic. Too dangerous."

"But no one knows what car we're driving," I said.

"It doesn't matter. The cameras are equipped with facial recognition. If they catch sight of us through the windshield, we'll get flagged."

"That news report last night said they hadn't identified any individual suspects," said Clara.

"You believe everything you see on TV?"

"No."

"There you go." Brooks reclined his seat a couple of notches and settled into it with a satisfied grunt. "Scraptown is a safer route out of the city. No cameras. No cops. Just an awful lot of folk with nowhere else to go and no opportunity to improve their lot in life."

"Why are these people even living like this?" I asked, looking out of the window with a mixture of disbelief and disgust. "Shouldn't the government be taking care of them?"

"Did the government of the world we rescued you from take care of their homeless situation?"

"Not really," I admitted. I had visited San Diego a few years ago and found myself in the middle of a tent city stretching along the sidewalks in one neighborhood I passed through. Hundreds of people living rough. It was a startling and disconcerting sight, but it was nothing compared to the squalor we were currently driving through, and I said as much. "But we don't have shantytowns outside of our major cities, either. At least, not in first-world countries."

"That must be nice," Brooks said. "But what makes you think a government will go out of their way to help the population of a shantytown when they won't even help an individual homeless person?"

"I never looked at it like that."

"The reason these places exist is because everyone turns a blind eye and lets the situation escalate until it gets out of hand. It will happen eventually anywhere that allows a single homeless person to stay that way. Blight breeds more blight. The problem isn't the world you live in. It's humanity in general. We are a flawed species."

"Why even bother creating alternate realities for people if those worlds will eventually disintegrate into what we see around us?" Clara asked. "Doesn't that feel kind of pointless to you?"

"Why does anyone do anything?" Brooks replied.

"Money," I said.

"Very good." Brooks turned to look at me. "They wrap the alternate realities in a veneer of humanitarianism. Saving the planet from overcrowding. Saving it from more pollution. Giving people a better place to live. But behind those good deeds lies a never-ending fountain of wealth."

"That's pretty cynical," Clara said.

"Not in the least." Brooks turned to face the front again, even though he wasn't doing any real driving. "It's the cold hard truth."

# CHAPTER TWENTY-FIVE

AFTER SCRAPTOWN, we slept for a while. Clara and I. The car's backseat was comfortable, plush, and we were exhausted. Clara could barely keep her eyes open. She laid her head on my shoulder and before long she was out. Her chest rose and fell as she snored lightly. If Brooks and Colt noticed, they said nothing. I tried to stay awake, tried to watch the unfamiliar landscape beyond my window roll by, but soon I drifted off as well.

When I awoke, the sun was high in the sky. A pale white disk visible through a dense layer of dull gray cloud cover that stretched featureless across the heavens before dropping to the horizon.

The city was far behind us now.

We were moving through a barren landscape that must once have been a lush green forest but was reduced to nothing more than a charred wasteland. Scorched tree trunks devoid of branches stood on each side of the road like a thousand silent sentinels, the ground beneath them thick with a layer of ash that blew across the road whenever the breeze caught it. Once in a while another vehicle passed us going the other way, but we were obviously on a little-used route.

"Welcome back," Brooks said from the front.

"Where are we now?" I asked, staring out of the window.

"Middle of nowhere an hour east of Pittsburgh," Brooks replied. "Taking the scenic route, if you can call it that, and keeping our heads down."

The car was still driving itself, which I found mildly disconcerting. Self-driving cars were nowhere near this advanced in the reality I remembered, and I had never ridden in one. The best I had managed was my brother's car in New York, which could parallel park itself. I even found that a bit unnerving. I didn't like the loss of control. This was on a whole other level.

"What happened to the trees in these parts?" I asked.

"Forest fire," Colt said. "Big one by the looks. We've been under drought warnings for the past two years. When it doesn't rain, the forests turn into a tinderbox. All it takes is one spark to wipe out a million acres."

Beside me, Clara was still sleeping. I tried not to move too much lest I disturb her. She needed the rest. "Are we stopping in Pittsburgh?" I asked.

"No. We'll cut a wide path around the city. If they are looking for us already back in Refuge City, we won't be safe in Pittsburgh either."

"Or any other big cities for that matter," Colt said.

Brooks yawned. Clara and I weren't the only ones who were tired. "We'll keep moving until dark. I know a place where we can stop for the night."

"Is it safe?" I asked.

"Safer than the city," came the reply.

"How are we going to make it all the way across the country if we have to avoid every major population center?" There were a lot of miles between us and the mysterious outpost called Fahrenheit near Lake Tahoe. It would take many days to get there, and we would need more provisions than Colt had managed to procure before we left.

"Let us worry about that," Brooks said.

Colt peered into the back. "Once we reach the Arizona Cauldron, it won't matter. There won't be any cities left to speak of. At least none with a population worth a damn."

"Where does that begin?"

"After St. Louis it gets barren in a hurry," Brooks replied. "Lots of dust storms that have pretty much wiped out the prairies."

"But it doesn't get really bad until you reach western Colorado and New Mexico. Think of Death Valley on a grand scale." Colt chuckled to himself. "Gotta say, I never thought I'd set foot near the place let alone drive all the way through it."

"First time for everything," Brooks said. He looked back at me, once again sending my heart racing until I remembered that he wasn't actually driving. "You getting hungry yet?"

My stomach growled in answer to his question, and I nodded. "Little bit."

"Great. Me too. I'll start looking for somewhere secluded to pull over and we'll eat."

Clara finally stirred. She opened her eyes and sat up, looking around. "How long was I out?"

Brooks answered. "Three or four hours. Going to stop for food up ahead. Sound good to you?"

"Sounds fantastic. I'm starving." Clara peered out of the window. She pulled a face. "Everywhere we go is worse than the last place."

"Forest fires," I told her.

She nodded and settled back in the seat. "I never thought I'd say this, but I miss that gas station in Vermont."

"And Walter, too?" I said with a grin, referring to her slimy weasel of a boss who turned into a crazy and tried to kill us before we were even properly introduced.

"Don't miss him so much," Clara said. "In fact, I don't miss him one little bit."

# CHAPTER TWENTY-SIX

WE FOUND a place to pull off the road and eat forty-five minutes later. An old logging trail that meandered into the wilderness and provided a perfect location to pause and stretch our legs far from prying eyes.

The scorched and burned landscape was in our rearview mirror and we were now surrounded by dense green forest that stretched in all directions.

Brooks navigated the logging trail for about a mile until we came to a small clearing with the remains of a stone building sitting in the middle. The roof was missing, and the windows were long gone, the spaces where they should have been nothing but dark, empty holes. The remains of a wooden porch sagged low to the ground; no doubt ate through with rot.

We pulled up under the shadow of the abandoned structure and climbed out of the car.

Colt dragged a cooler from the trunk. Inside was a selection of sandwiches Clara had made the previous evening before bed and packed ready for our trip. We sat on a fallen log at the edge of the clearing and ate, taking one assemblage each and sharing a family-sized bag of BBQ flavor chips. No one spoke until the last morsels of food had been consumed. With the meal finished, Clara stood up. "Hate to be crude, but I need to pee."

"Try the cabin," Brooks said.

Clara nodded and made her way across the clearing to the stone building. She climbed up onto the porch, treading carefully to make sure the rotten planks didn't give way underneath her. The front door was still there, but hanging half-open at an angle, stubbornly attached by one rusted hinge. She pushed her head in through the gap before climbing back down.

"That's a no-go," she said, shaking her head. "The entire roof has collapsed inside the building. Too much debris. I wouldn't want to risk climbing over it."

"Could be snakes in there, too," Colt warned her. "There's no one around. Go in the woods. That's what I'm planning to do."

Clara cast a wary eye toward the trees and back in my direction. "Will you come with me?"

"Sure." I stood up. "I could stand to go myself before we get back on the road."

Clara took my hand, and we set off, heading toward a narrow path that ran behind the cabin. We followed it for a minute or two until we were out of view before she stepped off the path and took care of business. I stood with my back turned. Once she was done, I went behind a tree and did the same.

We were about to head back when she stopped and looked around. "Do you hear that?"

"What?" I asked, scanning the underbrush between the trees to make sure we were truly alone.

"I hear running water."

Now that she mentioned it, I heard the water, too. A faint rush that sounded like it was coming from deep in the woods.

"Come on," Clara said grabbing my hand again. "It doesn't sound far away. Let's go see what it is."

"I think it might be better if we went back."

"Two minutes. A quick peek," Clara begged. "Everything in this world has been so drab and depressing. But look around. These woods remind you of home?"

"Little bit." She wasn't wrong. The air was fresh here, at least compared to the smoggy, fume-laden atmosphere of the city. The forest bloomed around in a burst of greenery, vibrant and natural. It wasn't exactly Vermont, but it tugged at my heartstrings, nonetheless.

"Well?" Clara looked at me with expectant eyes.

"Fine. Two minutes, and we go back."

"Thank you." She started off further down the path, pulling me along.

We climbed over a fallen tree that lay blocking the path and weaved around a large boulder that heaved out of the earth as if it were trying to escape. Soon the trees parted, and we found ourselves on the bank of a fast-flowing stream that cut through the wooded landscape like a serpentine ribbon. Branches overhung the water, some of them bowing low enough to touch the surface. Half-submerged rocks broke the stream's flow, creating miniature waterfalls that gurgled and bubbled. It was the opposite of everything else I had seen in this world. It made me feel normal for a moment.

Clara kicked off her shoes and pulled the legs of her jeans up to her knees. She took a step toward the water. "This place is perfection."

"Wait," I shouted, grabbing her arm and pulling her back at the last minute.

"What are you doing?" Clara turned to me with anger flashing in her eyes. "Can't you allow me a few minutes of normality before we have to get back in that car?"

"It's not that," I said, pointing toward the riverbank downstream, and the furry shape that lay unmoving at the water's edge. An unlucky animal that came to the stream for a drink and died. "Look."

Clara looked, and the angry expression on her face turned to one of fear. "That looks like a bear cub."

"Yes."

"Do you think the river water killed it?"

"A fair bet," I replied. Now that I looked closer, I saw more clues that the water was not what it appeared. A frothy white mucus-like substance had collected among the rocks at the edge of the stream. Further toward the middle, sulfurous yellow tendrils moved through the water like undulating, weaving snakes. "The pollution here must be off the charts."

The color had drained from Clara's face. "If I'd stepped in that stream…"

"You would've been wading through pure poison," I said, my gaze lingering on the deadly stream. "I think we've done enough sightseeing here. Let's head back."

Clara gave the landscape one last look, as if she were soaking up the false veneer of beauty all around us, before she slipped her shoes back on. "I hate this world."

"Me too." I took a step back toward the path. I hadn't made it more than a few feet when a low droning thrum filled the air, drowning out the chirp of insects and birdsong.

"What's that?" Clara asked.

"Good question." I froze and looked skyward. There was nothing but foliage and a patch of dreary sky above me.

"Sounds like it's getting closer."

And it did. The sound was getting louder and higher in pitch. A hum that did not sound natural.

I scanned our environment, searching for a clue regarding its origin.

Beside me, Clara gave a startled gasp.

"Look." She pointed along the stream, but it wasn't the dead animal carcass laying by the shore that she was looking at now. It was a cigar-shaped object hovering above the flowing water that caught her attention. It was smooth and silvery, slender, about a foot long. It reminded me of a big metallic pill. There was no visible method of propulsion. No protrusions spoiled its seamless surface. Yet it moved toward us anyway, gliding a good ten feet above the water's surface.

I stood transfixed for a moment, frozen by indecision. Should we run for the clearing or stay where we were and hope it would pass us by? I decided that fleeing would be the better option.

I grabbed Clara's hand and dragged her away from the riverbank toward the trail. But now the hum was getting louder. A shrill vibration that sliced through me, jarring and uncomfortable.

A mewling sound slipped from Clara's lips.

She raised her hands and pressed them against her ears.

I stumbled, almost fell. My vision became blurry.

The hum was all around us now. My head throbbed. I couldn't think.

I let go of Clara's hand.

She took another faltering step and pitched forward, falling to her knees.

I fought against the pain and tried to scoop her up, but it was no good. Because now I was collapsing right alongside her.

And above us, circling like a bird of prey, the silvery oblong pill.

# CHAPTER TWENTY-SEVEN

"WHAT'S HAPPENING TO US?" Clara's face was contorted in agony. She clawed the ground, fingers digging into the soft earth.

I tried to answer, but all that came out was a strangled gasp. The pain drilled through me. Reached inside my head and twisted my brain in knots. Flashes of bright light exploded before my eyes. My muscles spasmed and I flopped to one side, curling up like a fetus.

Consciousness slipped away. I wondered if I was going to die here, on the banks of a poisoned stream in a world I didn't remember.

Then another sound forced itself through the haze. A sharp crack from somewhere behind us. It echoed around the forest.

The hum stopped.

The pain receded like a tide drawing away from the shore.

I opened my eyes and waited for the dancing lights that flickered across my vision to burn themselves out.

A figure swam into focus.

Brooks.

And in his hands, he carried a gun that looked like something out of a science fiction movie.

Beside me, Clara groaned and raised her head. A trickle of blood pushed from her ear and ran down her jaw.

Brooks reached down and grabbed my arm. "Get up. We need to leave right now!"

"What the hell was that?" I struggled to stand. Shook my head to clear it of the last vestiges of brain fog. When I touched the side of my face, my fingers came away bloodied.

"Tracker drone."

I looked around, afraid the silvery oblong drone might renew its assault, but it wasn't hovering in the air anymore. It lay in the stream with a black and scorched hole in its smooth metallic shell.

Clara was standing now. She reached out and used my shoulder to steady herself. "I thought my head was going to explode."

"Neuro-disabler," Brooks said as if it was the most logical explanation in the world. "If there's one of those things around, there will be more. And worse. We have to get back to the car."

"Where did you get that?" I asked, looking at the gun.

"Where do you think?" Brooks was hustling us along the trail back to the clearing now. He glanced over his shoulder nervously and kept the gun held flat across his chest, finger close to the trigger. "It was in the trunk of the car. Colt procured it for us last night."

"You can just waltz into a store and buy something like that in this world?" I asked.

Brooks shot me a withering look. "Don't be ridiculous. Got it on the black market. We have friends in the illegal arms business."

"That doesn't sound very upstanding."

Brooks shrugged. "Sometimes you have to sleep with the devil."

We were approaching the clearing now. I could see Colt standing next to the car, waving to us. He pointed upwards and behind us, eyes wide and frantic.

I didn't have to search for the source of his consternation, because the hum was back. It was faint right now but building in intensity. A pulse of discomfort was already awakening somewhere deep inside my head.

It was either the same drone Brooks had disabled, which I found unlikely, given that it was in the river with a smoking hole in it from his gun, or the drone had a friend.

I risked a glance over my shoulder and wished I hadn't. There wasn't one drone bearing down on us now, but two. And they were gaining on us, zipping around the trees and swooping low.

The pulsing discomfort in my head was getting worse.

Clara cried out, her face twisting into a grimace.

"The car," Brooks shouted as we entered the clearing. "Get to the car quick as you can. The vehicle's metal body will disrupt the signal those drones are sending out. Make it more bearable."

I didn't need any urging.

We sprinted the final few yards. I did my best to ignore the crushing flares of pain that shot through my head like a thousand tiny daggers. My vision was blurring again. Pinpricks of light exploded in front of my eyes.

Colt was already in the driver's seat, waiting with his jaw clenched.

Brooks grunted and stumbled, then righted himself.

A tear ran down Clara's cheek.

The neurological weapons carried by the drones were affecting us all.

"Come on, guys. Hurry it up." Colt was sitting with one leg out of the vehicle. He had opened all the vehicle's doors already to make it easier for us.

I stumbled the last small distance, pushing Clara along in

front of me. When we reached the vehicle, I made sure she was inside before I climbed aboard next to her.

Brooks rounded the front of the car, turned, and took a potshot at the closest drone before climbing in.

This time he missed.

But it didn't matter. Colt was already slamming his foot on the accelerator and peeling out of the clearing at a breakneck pace even as we were closing the doors.

"Hold tight. I put the car in manual driver mode," he said over his shoulder. "It's going to get bumpy before it gets better."

The car sped up, blowing past the steady cruising speed we had maintained until now. Our ride up the logging trail into the clearing had been smooth and easy thanks to the car's self-driving system, but in manual mode at high speed, we bumped over every pothole and rut.

Brooks was right. The pain wasn't so bad now we were in the car. But it had not gone away, either.

I glanced through the rear window. Saw the drones zipping along behind us. We were going faster along the logging road than was probably safe, but the drones were moving faster still. Little by little, they were gaining on us. And as they did so, the pain levels inched higher.

Soon they would catch up to us, and then the pain would be too much to stand, even considering the car's protective metal shell that was acting like a sort of neurological faraday cage, dispersing the worst of the drone weapon's effects. When that happened Colt would either lose control and crash, or the car's automatic driving system would take over for him. Either way, it wouldn't matter, because we would probably be dead.

# CHAPTER TWENTY-EIGHT

CLARA PRESSED her hands to her ears again. She was sobbing. Desperate. "How can we make this stop."

"Only one way that I know of," Brooks said. He was cradling the gun on his lap. He glanced toward Colt. "You think you can keep her steady enough?"

"I can try." Colt reached up and drew his finger across a small oblong touchscreen near the rearview mirror. The screen lit up orange. The front section of the car's roof separated and slid back noiselessly. A concealed moonroof.

Brooks clutched the gun and unclipped his seatbelt. He pulled himself up and out so that he was standing on the seat with his top half out through the hole in the roof.

The car bumped sideways and swerved back onto the road.

Brooks cursed. "I thought you were going to hold it steady."

"Doing my best down here," colt shot back. "It's not easy driving when it feels like your head's about to pop. Hurry up and take care of those drones."

"That's the plan." Brooks positioned the bulky rifle, using the top of the car to steady it. He dropped down behind the gun sights and aimed. When he pulled the trigger there was a sharp crack.

The lead drone pitched sideways to avoid his fire, then righted itself again.

Brooks cursed again. "Missed."

"You need some help up there?" I asked. The drones were smart. They were learning to anticipate.

"Wouldn't turn it down. Open the middle section of seat in between you and Clara. You'll be able to reach into the trunk. There's another gun in there."

I did as I was told and tugged at the seat. The center section dropped down and I was able to reach in and fumble around in the trunk until my hand closed over a cold metallic object. It was another gun like the one Brooks was using.

I worked through the pain in my head, ignored those dancing lights in front of my eyes. I only hoped I could see well enough to shoot. It took me a few seconds to wriggle my way up and out of the seat before I was able to join Brooks. With two of us half out of the car, it was tight. The side of the moonroof pressed against me, cutting into my stomach.

Brooks reached across and swiped his finger across a small touchscreen on the side of the gun. "Safety's off now. Point and shoot."

"Whatever you say." The gun was heavy in my hands.

Brooks was taking aim again. "When I shoot, I want you to fire at the same time, about twelve inches to the left."

"What if the drone veers right?"

"Then we both miss," Brooks said, "so hope that it doesn't."

"Sure thing."

"On my mark."

I waited. Took aim to the left of Brooks. He counted down from three. Reached one. "Now!"

I pressed down on the trigger at the same time Brooks took his shot.

The drone weaved to one side and straight into my own line of fire. It swung upward, tried to right itself. Brooks took the opportunity to take a second shot. This one hit the drone in its underbelly. A small hole opened up in the machine's outer shell. A Puff of smoke curled into the air and the drone pitched away from us in a crazy death roll then disappeared into the foliage on the side of the road.

But there was still one more drone chasing us.

"Same again," Brooks ordered.

Without counting down this time, he pressed the trigger and fired.

I followed suit, taking a shot at the same position as before.

This drone wasn't falling for it. Instead of sliding sideways to avoid the gunfire, it shot straight up into the sky and disappeared from view.

"Where did it go?" I asked, looking for the silhouette of the shiny metallic machine against the cloudy gray firmament.

"Somewhere we can't shoot at it," Brooks replied. "It will be back."

Of that, I was sure. Because it hadn't gone far. I could still hear the high-pitched hum of the drone's neurological weapon. Could still feel the needles of pain digging into my brain. I gazed skyward, trying to find the elusive machine, looked down at the woods and the road behind us.

"Crap." Below us, Colt let forth with a string of curses.

"It's in our path," Brooks shouted over the roar of wind buffeting the vehicle.

And there it was. Ahead of us on the road, barreling forward in a deadly game of chicken.

The car juddered and slowed down as Colt slammed on the brakes. Brooks fired at the drone. Once, twice, three times.

I did the same.

"Better hang on, I'm losing it," colt screamed from below.

I thought he meant the drone, at least until the car took a

sickening lurch and veered to one side. The back fishtailed and spun around.

There was time for one more shot as the drone passed across my field of view.

My bullet caught it dead center, more by luck than good judgment.

The drone tumbled away out of sight.

Brooks was already scrambling back into the car, dragging me down with him. He threw the gun at his feet and buckled his seatbelt.

I fell into the back, landing hard as the car's front wheels left the road.

I struggled to buckle myself in, fought against the car's inertia. The buckle clicked home in the nick of time.

There was a sickening moment of weightlessness. My stomach rose into my throat. The front of the vehicle dropped hard into a ditch and stopped while the rear kept going.

A weird and random thought rattled through my bruised mind. Something a physics teacher said during science class when I was a kid. It was Newton's first law. An object in motion wants to stay in motion.

The car was proving this concept to me in real time. The back end somersaulted into the air, rear wheels spinning against nothing but air. For a second, the car stayed upright like a steel monolith, and I thought it would right itself, but then the vehicle continued its arc and crashed down onto its roof. Broken glass sprayed into the cabin. There was a squeal of tortured metal. Clara screamed. Then there was nothing.

# CHAPTER TWENTY-NINE

THE WORLD FLUTTERED in and out. Brief snatches of consciousness followed by a void of painless relief. I clawed my way back toward reality. Opened my eyes.

The car was upside down and off the road. A thick tree branch had skewered the empty space where the windshield used to be. I pushed foliage out of the way and tried to find Clara.

Then she found me.

A hand pushed past the branch and touched my shoulder. When she spoke, there was a groggy edge to her voice. "Hayden. You still alive over there?"

"So far as I can tell." I could see Brooks and Colt moving in the front, hanging upside down from their seatbelts. Miraculously, none of us had ended up impaled by the tree.

"We can't stay here," Colt said. He unclipped his seatbelt and half fell, half slid onto the car's upturned roof. "Those drones weren't here alone."

"Why were they here in the first place?" Brooks asked. He unclipped his own seatbelt, then maneuvered himself upright and pushed at his door, but it wouldn't open.

"A good question." Colt had a shoulder against the driver's door. With some effort, he pried it open and crawled out.

Then he was at the back of the car, pulling on the rear door and freeing me.

I climbed from the vehicle and checked myself for broken bones. To my relief, everything was in the same place as before the car had left the road. Better yet, the mind-numbing pain inflicted upon us by the drones was gone. The only evidence left behind was a dried trickle of blood near my ear. I wondered what the drone's neurological weapon had been doing to me to make me bleed like that. I was still functioning and could think clearly again now, so I decided I didn't want to know the answer.

I looked around. We were still on the logging trail, but it couldn't be far to the road given how fast Colt had been driving. Neither of the drones was visible.

Brooks and Clara had extricated themselves from the wrecked vehicle now, too. We were the luckiest people on earth. Not only had we avoided being impaled by the tree, but none of us appeared to have sustained any serious injuries in the crash. The car, however, was a goner.

"What are we going to do now?" Clara asked. "We don't have any wheels."

"We're going to do the only thing we can," Brooks replied. "Use our feet and look for an alternate ride as soon as possible."

"I'll get the supplies." Colt went to the back of the vehicle and started fighting with the trunk lid.

Brooks went to the cabin and retrieved the two guns. "Don't want to lose these. I have a feeling we're going to need them again."

"And soon." Colt had pried the trunk open and was now grabbing provisions and stuffing them into four backpacks. There were other items too. A pair of tents. Camping equipment. He gathered it all together, then threw one bag at me and gave another to Clara. "We're going to have to carry everything."

Colt slipped a third bag onto his shoulders and handed Brooks the last one. "First order of business. We need to get away from the crash site."

Brooks shook his head. "Not yet. We have some other business to attend to first."

"Sir?" Colt raised an eyebrow.

"This wasn't some random encounter. Those drones, and whoever sent them, knew exactly where we were."

"That's impossible," Colt said. "No one knew what vehicle we were driving, and even if they did, we couldn't be tracked. I disabled the global positioning on the car before we left."

"They weren't tracking the car." Brooks was looking at Clara and me.

"Hold on a minute," I replied, the anger evident in my tone. "You think we led those things to you?"

"Not on purpose." Brooks hoisted the gun strap over his shoulder. "Undress."

"What?" Had I heard him right? Was my mind still scrambled by those silver flying devils?

"Take your clothes off. Both of you."

"Not happening." Clara shook her head.

"Don't be so obstinate. One or both of you is implanted with a tracker. We need to find it."

"Well, it's not me," Clara said. "I'm not even anything to do with this One World group. I got caught up in all of this by accident."

"I'd rather be safe than sorry," Brooks said. His hand was resting on the rifle strap. I wondered if he was going to unsling it and force us to strip at gunpoint.

"Let's all take it easy, okay?" I stepped between Brooks and Clara. "I'll undress, and you can check me first."

"All right. Get on with it. Every minute we stay here is one minute less that we have to escape before the people behind those drones show up."

I nodded and undressed. When I was down to my skivvies, I raised my arms. "There. Happy?"

"We need the rest of it, too."

"Really?" I dropped my boxers.

"You," Brooks said, nodding toward Clara. "Check him for scars. Look for something about an inch long. They won't put it anywhere obvious."

Clara looked at me. Her cheeks flushed. "Sorry about this."

"It's okay," I said. "We're not exactly strangers to each other."

"Never thought I'd be checking you out like this, though," Clara said as a malicious smile curled her lips.

"Me either." I waited while Clara examined me.

She started at my shoulders and worked her way down. When she found nothing at the front, she moved to my back. After a while, she let out an exclamation. "Found something."

"Let me see." Brooks stepped around me.

Clara's fingers brushed my right butt cheek. She was talking to Brooks. "Look here. There's a scar like the one you described."

"You know anything about a scar down here?" Brooks asked me.

"No. Can't say that I do."

"This is what we're looking for." Brooks laid the gun on the ground and reached into his pocket. I saw him remove a sleek silver penknife. He looked up at me. "This is going to hurt, I'm afraid."

He didn't need to tell me what he was going to do. It was obvious. "Hurry up and get on with it."

"Fair enough. You might want to grit your teeth."

Before I could answer, the penknife dug into my flesh. Despite my best efforts, I couldn't help a low grunt. Then

Brooks was standing up, wiping my blood off his knife blade. He held up a tiny metallic object. It was an oblong cylinder less than an eighth of an inch wide and a quarter inch long. "All done."

I looked at the minuscule object. "They were tracking us with that?"

"Must have been implanted when the authorities caught you. It's probably been there since before you were sent into the alternate reality. Security in case you ever made it back to the real world."

"I like this place less and less with every passing minute." I pulled my clothes back on. "Can we get out of here now?"

Brooks flicked the tracker off into the foliage at the side of the road. He turned his attention to Clara. "Not yet. We have one more person to search."

# CHAPTER THIRTY

"Not going to happen," I said, ready for a fight. "We found the tracker."

"We found a tracker," Brooks corrected me. "Doesn't mean there isn't another one."

"What about the two of you?" I looked between Brooks and Colt. "How do I know one of you isn't implanted?"

"Because neither of us has been arrested."

"Clara hasn't been arrested, either." I pointed out.

"But she did have her name pulled for the Great Migration."

"So what?"

"She underwent a memory wipe and replacement. They might have chipped her at the same time," Colt said. "We need to check."

I realized they weren't going to take no for an answer. "All right. Fine. But I'll check her for implants. The two of you either go somewhere else or turn your backs."

"You have three minutes, then we need to get out of here," Brooks said. He nudged Colt and the two of them wandered further down the road.

I turned to Clara. "You ready to do this?"

"Let's get it over with." She started to undress. "You better not tease me about this later."

"What, me?" I feigned indignation. "I'm a perfect gentleman."

"Yeah. You kind of are," Clara said as she slipped the last of her clothes off and stood in front of me with her arms at her sides. "Which is why I'm hoping you won't take too long with this. It's embarrassing enough without the others returning before I get dressed."

"Don't worry, I'll be quick." And I was. Because I didn't believe for one second Clara had been implanted with any kind of tracking device. There would be no reason to do that. Me, on the other hand . . . I was a threat.

By the time the others returned, Clara was dressed again.

"She's clean," I said. "No recent scars. No trackers."

"Happy now?" She glared at Brooks.

"We had to be sure." Brooks looked back up the trail toward the clearing. I wondered if he was scanning for more drones. Thankfully, none had appeared. I wasn't sure if I could take another onslaught by their neurological weapons.

"Where do we go from here?" I asked, my eyes drifting to the ruined vehicle sitting on its roof at the side of the road.

"We walk to the nearest town." Colt didn't look happy.

Neither did Clara. "How far away is that?"

Brooks shrugged. "Saw a sign back before we turned onto the logging trail. Said there was a place called Happenstance fifteen miles distant."

"That far?" Clara's face dropped. "That's a long way to walk."

"Which is why we should get moving," Brooks said.

"Not to mention that the owners of those drones can't be too far away," Colt added. "I'd rather not be here when they show up."

"Me either," I agreed. If the drones inflicted that much

pain, I couldn't imagine what the people who controlled them would do to us.

"Let's get the hell out of here." Clara picked up her backpack and pushed past Brooks and Colt. She started down the trail without looking back. I had a feeling it was going to be a while before she was ready to forgive them.

Brooks looked at me. "She's got some fire in her gut."

"You would do well not to forget it," I told him. "She's tough. We went through a lot on the other side before you found us."

"I have no doubt," Brooks said. "Look, Like I said, we had to—"

"Hey, I get it. Don't worry." I hoisted my backpack over my shoulders and followed Clara. "Besides, I'm not the one you have to worry about. You humiliated her."

"That wasn't my intention."

"Then maybe you should apologize to Clara, not me."

"I will." Brooks nodded. "But not right now. We have bigger problems."

Colt glanced around nervously. "We'll never make it to Happenstance before dark. It's too far."

"Which means we'll have to find somewhere to bed down for the night," Brooks said. "And we'll be walking most of tomorrow, too."

"We can't use the road," Colt said. "We'll be too easy to spot."

"Which is why we're going to cut through the woods." Brooks didn't look happy. "That will slow us down, but the trees will also provide cover."

I voiced a thought that had been forming at the back of my mind. "Those people that want us dead—that senator woman and her cronies—will expect us to head for the nearest town."

"Probably."

"But it can't be helped," Brooks said. "We need transportation and that's the closest place to get it."

"And if they are waiting for us there?"

"Let's deal with one problem at a time, shall we?" Brooks picked up the pace to catch up to Clara.

Up ahead was the intersection with the road we were traveling before we pulled off. But Brooks wasn't heading there. Instead, he steered us off the trail and into the forest. Now all we had to do was navigate fifteen miles of rough wooded terrain and then deal with whatever awaited us at the other end.

I only hoped we weren't marching toward our own deaths.

# CHAPTER THIRTY-ONE

WE WALKED through the woods for five hours, putting as much distance as we could between ourselves and the wrecked vehicle. At sunset, Brooks found a shady area surrounded by Oak and poplar trees in which to spend the night. We were all tired. Clara looked like she might not be up to taking another step. My feet were hurting, and I can only imagine hers were, too.

Colt had the foresight to secure a pair of small tents when he was out gathering supplies the previous evening. He also packed a compact propane stove and a device that he called an atmospheric extractor. It could provide clean drinking water simply by dragging molecules out of the air. I was skeptical, but he assured us it would work. After seeing the pollution of the riverbank, I was grateful for this device.

We couldn't guarantee to find suitable and safe shelter each night, so the plan had always been to camp out if necessary. Now that we had lost the car, we had no choice, at least until we found another ride.

Having decided on our campsite, we set to work and were soon sitting around a roaring fire with the tents erected in the background. Clara and I would take one, while Brooks and

Colt would share the other. It was going to be a tight fit, but I wasn't complaining. I liked my tent companion. Brooks and Colt didn't feel the same way, I was sure.

After we ate, Clara asked a question that had been on my mind as well.

"If there was a tracking device implanted in Hayden, how come we got so far before they came after us?"

Brooks warmed his hands over the fire. "The senator reached out to me a few hours after we brought Hayden back from the alternate universe. She said there was evidence that would prove the government knew about the collapsing universes. My guess is they used her to draw Hayden out rather than risk creating a scene in the center of the city."

"But the senator was on your side up to that point, wasn't she?"

"She was, but I'm willing to bet that she was compromised way before Hayden reappeared. She was being kept as an ace."

"All those meetings we had with her," Colt said. "How much of what we told her got back to the government?"

"Depends how early she switched allegiances," Brooks said. "Either way, they held her back until they needed her."

"Okay. They intended for that creature to kill Hayden and the rest of us in the warehouse. I get that," Clara said. "But they must have known their plan had failed pretty quickly. They waited another twenty-four hours before doing anything else."

"They didn't wait. They blew up our headquarters." Brooks clenched his fists. "The senator can't have been the only person who betrayed us. That bomb didn't get in there by magic."

"We may never know who planted it," said Colt.

"The bomb wasn't meant for us though," I said. "They didn't want my body to be found in that building because it would raise questions. I'm supposed to be in an alternate dimension. That's why they lured us to the warehouse first."

"It was a double strike. One to eliminate the leadership and Hayden, and another to discredit the organization and make us look like terrorists," said Brooks. "That's why they waited until now to come after us with those drones. They need to eliminate Hayden quietly. Out of sight."

"They almost did," I said. My head didn't hurt now, but I could still feel the aftereffects of the neurological weapon. It was like having a mild hangover. I didn't exactly feel bad, but I didn't feel right, either. I hoped it would go away soon. "You think there are people back where we crashed the car, looking for us right now?"

"No. By now, they will have cleaned that up and eliminated any trace of what occurred. They know we've moved on. But I guarantee they're looking for us."

"At least we've made it harder for them," I said. My butt still throbbed where Brooks had gouged out the tracker with the tip of his penknife. I hoped he hadn't done too much damage down there. "They can't track me now."

"They should never have been able to track you in the first place." Brooks scowled, clearly angry at himself. "We should have checked you for tracking devices the minute we brought you back. It was a stupid mistake that almost got us killed."

"But it didn't," I said. "And the tracker is gone."

"Doesn't mean they'll give up," Brooks said. "These are dangerous people we're messing with. People who have a lot to lose. They'll stop at nothing to silence us."

Colt stared at Brooks across the fire. "I'll be glad when we reach the Arizona Cauldron. No one will follow us in there."

"You sure about that?" Brooks asked, his eyebrows raising.

Colt gave this some consideration and shook his head. "No. I'm really not."

# CHAPTER THIRTY-TWO

WE SET off early the next morning. We still had a trek of at least eleven miles ahead of us. The woods were tough going. Back in the other universe, I had taken up hiking and was accustomed to walking through the wilderness. It would have only taken me four or five hours to cover such a distance in the rolling green hills of Vermont. But here every step was treacherous. There were roots and vines underfoot. Prickly bushes and fallen logs.

At one point, we came to a brook that looked very much like the one where we had first encountered the drones. The pollution in the water was obvious, although there were no dead animals on the bank this time. I wondered if it was the same watercourse, and we were downstream. It was impossible to know. It was also in our way. Having seen the dead bear cub, I had no desire to wade through it.

But there was no choice. It was that or turn back, which was not an option.

Brooks went first. He was wearing sturdy boots and navigated his way across, balancing on boulders that protruded from the water's surface.

Clara went next, following his instructions and stepping from stone to stone. She arrived at the far bank, mostly dry.

After that, it was my turn, and then Colt brought up the rear. We stood on the other bank while Brooks used a compass to get our bearings. It was a low-tech solution in a world of fancy gadgets, but it was also safe, as Colt explained. If it didn't contain electronics, nobody could track it.

We set off again, plodding through the dense understory until my legs were scratched raw despite my jeans. There was little conversation. We were all exhausted, not to mention on edge. And it was a good thing too, or we wouldn't have noticed the approach of another drone.

It was a barely perceptible noise. A faint buzz like an angry fly. But Brooks knew exactly what it was.

"Down," he barked the command before the rest of us even had time to react.

I dropped to the ground near a thorny, tangled bush and pulled Clara down with me.

Brooks and Colt scrambled for cover beside us.

The drone came into view, gliding between the trees, smooth and almost noiseless. A sleek silver metallic deadly football. It approached us at a slow pace.

Clara nudged me and whispered. "It's going to find us."

"Stay down and keep quiet," I replied.

The drone was close now. It paused and rotated in the air ten feet from where we were hiding. I got the impression it was scanning the environment.

Brooks stiffened next to me. He was clutching the gun but hadn't raised it yet. I knew why. If there was one drone, there might be more. And even if we took this one out, it wouldn't do us any good. We would reveal our location to whoever was pursuing us and we didn't have the luxury of a vehicle to help us escape this time.

I held my breath.

The drone hovered for a moment, then kept going. It passed by us without stopping and was soon lost in the trees.

I released the air from my lungs slowly. "I think it's gone."

Clara must have been holding her breath, too, because I heard her exhale. "That was too close."

"Come on, let's move." Brooks started through the undergrowth, pushing branches aside. He stayed low and glanced skyward every now and again. "If there's one drone around, there could be more."

"How did they even find us again?" Clara asked. "We got rid of the tracker."

"They haven't found us." Brooks had broken cover and was moving fast now, pushing on through the woods like a man on a mission. Every once in a while, he glanced up. His gun was at the ready. "If they had, we wouldn't have escaped so easily."

"That's why the drone didn't incapacitate us with its neurological weapon," I said. "They didn't know we were there."

"Precisely. If I had to guess, the drone was running a grid pattern search," Brooks said.

Colt agreed with him. "Senator Kane and the Senate Multiverse Committee must be pretty mad they lost us yesterday. Sending drones over such a wide area. I bet there's more. We should proceed with caution."

"You still think we should make for Happenstance now we know they're still looking for us?" I asked. "If I was the senator, I would assume we were heading for the nearest town. It would make sense."

"Especially since we lost our ride," Clara said.

"I've been giving that some thought," Brooks said. "Happenstance makes the most sense. The next closest town is at least another twenty miles further. We don't have the supplies or energy to make it that far on foot. Happenstance is our only option."

"And it could also be our downfall," I said. "There's no way the senator won't have people waiting for us."

"Which is why we're going to do this the smart way," Brooks said. "I have no intention of waltzing into town and strolling down Main Street like a bunch of tourists. When we reach the outskirts, we'll find somewhere to lie low. Then we'll get what we need."

"Like more food and water, and a new vehicle," Colt said.

I was about to ask how we would accomplish that, but as I pushed past a dense shrub, my foot snagged a low branch and I tripped, almost falling. I stumbled forward.

Brooks reached out and steadied me. "You alright, there?"

"Fine," I replied, composing myself, then returned to my question. "How are we going to get another car?"

"Same way we got the guns," Brooks replied.

"The black market," I said.

"Exactly. Which means talking to my contacts back in Refuge City. I'll need to call in some favors. I'd rather not do it, but I don't think we have any choice."

"Our backs are against the wall," Colt agreed. "Nothing else we can do."

"In the meantime, we keep walking," Brooks said. "And let's cut the chitter chatter. Keep our wits about us. We still have several miles to cover, and if we run into another drone, I'd like to see the damned thing before it sees us."

# CHAPTER THIRTY-THREE

WE CAME upon the town of Happenstance as the sun was sliding low on the horizon. For the last hour of our trek, we had been walking on steadily rising and increasingly rough terrain. My first glimpse of Happenstance came from above as we crested the peak of a rocky prominence and looked down across a wooded hillside into the valley below.

The town sprawled out around a glistening river that weaved through the heart of the valley. There was a downtown area with three and four-story brick buildings nestled close to a bridge that connected the riverbanks. Further away were larger buildings that looked like warehouses and factories. Residential neighborhoods fanned out from the town center and crept up the low slopes of the valley.

A single strip of dark asphalt stretched away from town in both directions. Had we not lost the vehicle, this would have been the way we approached Happenstance, no doubt.

"Looks quiet from up here," I said as we came to a halt and gazed down into the valley. The place reminded me of a hundred old mill towns I had driven through on journeys back and forth between Vermont and New York, where my brother

Jeff lived—or at least, the brother I was given in the false narrative of my life that the government of this world supplanted in place of my real memories.

"Looks can be deceptive," Brooks replied.

"There's a welcoming party waiting for us down there," Colt grumbled. "I can pretty much guarantee it."

"So, how do you want to do this?" I asked, shooting Brooks a sideways glance.

"First thing we have to do is find accommodation," Brooks said. "Somewhere safe to spend the night. I'd rather not spend a second night in a tent."

Colt rubbed his neck. "Especially if there are drones scouting the area, which I guarantee there will be since this is the closest town to where we left the car."

"After we have a place to lay our heads, I'll make a call or two," Brooks said. "Try and arrange us some wheels so we can be out of town before anyone knows we were even there. We'll need more provisions, too. Food and water for the next leg of the trip."

"Agreed," said Colt. "We should stock up now before we reach the Cauldron. There won't be many places to find supplies there."

"Right." Brooks nodded.

"You still haven't answered my question," I told Brooks. "How are we going to accomplish all of that without ending up caught or dead?"

"Very carefully." Brooks looked grim. He took a step forward. "Come on. Time's wasting. Let's get down there. I don't know about the rest of you, but I won't be able to relax until we're inside out of sight."

"Wait." I gripped his arm. A thought had occurred to me. "What about the guns? We can't walk into town with them over our shoulders."

"Good point. We'll conceal the weapons on the lower

slope. When we're ready to move on I'll send someone back to retrieve them."

"I don't relish the idea of going in there unarmed," Colt said.

"Neither do I, my friend." Brooks rested a hand on Colt's shoulder. "But there's no choice."

# CHAPTER THIRTY-FOUR

IT TOOK another hour to descend into the valley and reach the outskirts of Happenstance. We made our way towards the downtown area, keeping our heads low and walking apart to make it less obvious that we were together. Brooks went first, walking ahead on his own. I walked by Clara's side with my arm around her shoulder. A young couple out for an evening stroll. Colt came last, trailing far enough behind us to be unobtrusive, but not so far that he lost sight of the group. Anyone passing by would not look twice at us, especially as we got closer to downtown, and there were more people about.

We had stashed the guns behind a large boulder partway down the slope and covered them with brush and leaves. It was far off the beaten track and there was little chance anyone would come across them, especially since we were hoping to retrieve them the next morning and be on our way. Both Brooks and Colt looked uneasy being unarmed. If we ran into trouble, there would be no way to defend ourselves. But it was a chance we must take. Camping in the woods above town was too dangerous. Our tents would draw the attention of any drone that came along, and we knew that Senator Kane and those she worked for had sunk considerable resources into finding us. I wondered what cover story they had provided. A hunt for the Refuge City terrorists, perhaps? That seems like the most likely excuse. Not that it mattered. We wouldn't be safe out in the wilds. I only hoped we would be safe enough in town.

We found what Brooks believed to be suitable accommodation on the edge of downtown. A rundown motel that could have been any of a thousand such places I had passed by while driving down East Coast interstates. It looked old and drab. Tired.

We stood on the corner of the block and discussed our options.

"This will do fine," Brooks said, studying the motel's outdated façade.

There were several vehicles in the parking lot, mostly in spaces right outside of the rooms, and a few trucks parked across several bays at the edge of the lot. A sign in the lobby window announced vacancies.

"Doesn't look any different to a roach motel in our reality," Clara said with a touch of surprise.

"Why would it?" Brooks replied. "Place is probably a hundred years old and hasn't been renovated more than twice since it was built."

"I always imagined the future to be better."

"Have you seen much that looks better anywhere else since we plucked you out of that collapsing reality?" Brooks asked.

"Not really," Clara admitted.

"And anyway, this isn't the future. It's the present. Technically, the reality you were living in was based on the past."

"Still a disappointment," Clara said. "Kind of hoped there wouldn't be flea pit motels anymore."

"You should be glad there is," Brooks said. "The people who run places like this don't pay too much attention to the guests. Not like the fancy places. We'll go unnoticed here if we are careful."

"At least, that's the plan," Colt said.

"I hate to break up the party," I said. "But maybe we could continue this chat later, once we're not on the streets."

"You're right." Brooks cleared his throat. "Room first. Then we can debate how little things change."

"Let's get it over with," I said, taking a step forward.

"Wait." Brooks stopped me. "We can't all go in there. This might be a flea pit, but I'd rather not show our faces if we don't have to."

"I'll go in alone," Colt said. "I can be in and out before—"

"No." Brooks cut him off. "We need someone less noticeable. Someone who won't draw attention."

Clara's hand touched mine. "Sounds like you're talking about me."

"You must be a mind reader," Brooks said. "Exactly what I was thinking."

"That's a terrible idea." I looked at Clara. "There is no way in hell I'm letting you go in there alone. We'll go in together, posing as a couple."

"That won't work," Brooks said. "If they have cameras in the lobby, you'll be exposed. The authorities might track us here. The same goes for me and Colt. They know us. And for all we know, our faces are all over the news by now. The desk clerk might recognize us. There's less chance anyone has identified Clara. She wasn't on the radar. They don't know her name or that we brought her back over. With luck, they don't even have a clear image of her from the bombing site."

"The senator got a good look at her in that warehouse," I said.

"That's true. But we never introduced her. Everything went wrong too quickly. I'm sure there were no cameras. Senator Kane wouldn't want a record of her transgressions. As far as anyone else is concerned, she's nobody." Brooks drew in a long breath. "Clara's our best option. And we'll be right outside, waiting around the corner. If anything happens, we'll know."

"And it might be too late by then." I wasn't relenting on this. I got Clara into this situation, and I intended to keep her safe.

"Hayden." Clara glared at me. "It's not your decision to make."

"Like hell, it isn't."

"So now you're my boss?" Clara's voice rose in pitch. I could see the anger behind her eyes.

"I never said that." This was getting out of hand. We didn't have the time. "I'm looking out for you. It's not safe."

"It hasn't been safe ever since the gas station. We all have to take risks if we're going to survive. This is my risk. And as Jason said, it's a small one. No one even knows who I am." She looked at Brooks. "I'm ready. Let's do this."

# CHAPTER THIRTY-FIVE

"She can't go in there as is," Colt said. "Her presence will trip security protocols right away. She's not even supposed to be in this world anymore."

"I'm aware of that," Brooks answered. He reached into his pocket and removed a small, flat box. He opened it. Inside sat what looked like a pair of contact lenses in a pair of fluid-filled compartments. He turned to Clara. "I was hoping to save these in case we needed them further into the trip, but we have no choice."

"Contact lenses?" Clara said. "What do they do, change my eye color?"

"Not quite. This is a cashless society, but you'll still have to pay for the room. These will allow you to do so without being flagged in any government systems."

"I don't understand." Clara looked at the box.

"Neither do I," I said.

Colt stepped in. "It's simple. The hotel will use biometrics, namely a retina scan, to confirm your identity and charge you for the room. Put these lenses in your eyes, and they will trick the scanner into thinking you are someone else."

"Who?"

"It doesn't matter," Brooks said. "A hacked identity."

"That's the real reason none of us could go in except Clara," I said, realizing why Brooks was so adamant that it must be her who booked the motel room. "You need a woman because it's a female identity programmed into those lenses."

"Yes," Brooks replied. "But not for the reason you think. The payment system isn't very sophisticated. Doesn't need to be. It reads the iris and charges whatever payment account is associated with it. The system doesn't care whether you're male or female, old or young. But it will make a reservation using whatever name is associated with the hacked identity. In this case, a woman called Edwina Clay. We might be able to fool the biometrics, but if a man walks in and makes a reserva-tion in a woman's name, that will be a red flag."

"Why do you even have those?" I asked, looking down at the lenses. "And why a female identity? A man would've made more sense."

"We had no choice. Colt got them at the same time he acquired the guns. We took what we were offered. If Clara wasn't along for the ride, we couldn't use them."

"Okay, I get it," Clara said. "I put the contacts in and become someone else, at least in the digital world. Then I take them out again, and I'm back to myself."

"Not quite…" Brooks hesitated, as if he didn't want to say the next bit.

"Spit it out," I said.

"You don't take the contacts out again. Once you place them in your eyes, they get absorbed. They alter your retinas for a period. A day, maybe two. Then the effects wear off."

"One use only," I said.

"Yes. Which is why I was hoping to save them for later. We don't have anymore."

"It was hard enough getting hold of one pair," Colt said.

"Can we get on with it," Clara said. "I'd like to get this over with."

"All right." Brooks held the box out. "There's one more thing."

"What?" I had a feeling I wasn't going to like this. I was right.

"It's going to hurt a bit, at least at first." Brooks looked uncomfortable.

"Define *hurt a bit*," Clara said.

"It won't be pleasant. But it will only be painful for five or ten seconds as your eyes absorb the contacts."

"Wonderful." Clara took the box. "What do I need to do?"

"You ever put contact lenses in before?"

"No."

"Is easy. Pick up the lens on the tip of your finger, hold your head back, and slide the lens onto your eyeball. After that, it's all automatic."

"I'll give it a try," Clara said.

"Better do them both quickly, one after the other," Colt told her. "Once it starts to hurt, you may not want to put the second one in otherwise."

"This keeps getting better." Clara bit her lip. "You ever done this?"

"Once, a long time ago. Which is why I'm glad I don't have to do it now."

"You're not selling me on this." Clara reached into the box with a finger and plucked out one of the lenses. She lifted her head back and put it into her eye. She winced and blinked, then took the second lens and did the same. After a moment, she looked at Brooks. "This isn't so bad. It really doesn't hurt so—"

The pain hit her all at once. The words died in her throat. She gave a strangled cry and doubled over. Tears streamed down her cheeks. She gasped, her hands clenching into fists, fingernails digging into her palms.

Several seconds passed.

I stood by in helpless silence and watched her battle the pain.

After a while her breathing slowed and returned to normal. She straightened and wiped the tears from her cheeks.

"You okay?" Brooks asked.

"Let's get this thing done," Clara replied, her voice strained. "And next time you need a volunteer, count me out."

# CHAPTER THIRTY-SIX

WE WAITED out of sight in the doorway of a closed-down store with *going out of business* signs plastered on the windows while Clara went into the motel office. Before she left, Brooks had instructed her to book only one room with two queen beds. That way, there would be no questions about occupancy.

She had been gone for a while, and I was getting concerned. What if something had gone wrong and her true identity had been discovered? I half expected to hear sirens and see police converging upon the motel, eager to apprehend one of the Refuge City bombers.

"What's taking her so long?" I asked, stepping out from the doorway, and looking toward the motel after ten minutes had passed. "How long does it take to book a room in this reality? She should be back by now."

"She'll be back soon, I'm sure," Brooks said. "Relax."

That was easier said than done. "And if she's not?"

"Let's worry about that if it happens."

"I should go look for her." I wasn't much in the mood to wait around.

"Not going to happen. You'll be on camera the minute you step into that lobby. If the authorities ever come sniffing around, they will know we were here." There was an air of authority in Brooks' voice.

"You keep telling me what to do, yet you claim I was your leader," I told him.

"And you don't remember any of that, which doesn't make you a very effective leader right at this moment."

I couldn't argue with that logic.

Not that it mattered. Colt had another reason not to follow Clara into the motel office. "Brooks is right. We can't afford to be seen on camera if we can help it. But we also can't risk the desk clerk recognizing you. We don't know if our identities have been released in association with the bombing."

"Fine, I'll stay outside. But let me go check on her."

"If she isn't back soon, I'll consider it," Brooks conceded.

It was better than nothing, yet as the minutes ticked away I grew more concerned. Eventually, I decided enough was enough. "That's it. I'm going whether you like it or not."

Colt stepped in front of me, blocking my path. "No, you're not."

"Get out of my way," I said, ready to push past him, if necessary. But then, as I was about to act, Clara came around the corner with a grin on her face. I breathed a sigh of relief. Backed away from Colt.

"I did it," she said, oblivious to the tense situation. "One room with two queen beds on the bottom floor."

"Good job," Brooks said, looking pleased. "You have any trouble?"

"Not a bit."

"What took you so long, then?" I asked.

"There was someone ahead of me. Another couple booking a room. Didn't want to spend any longer than necessary inside the office so I waited outside until they were finished, which took a while. Don't know why." Her grin widened. "Those contacts worked like a charm. The guy booked me in under the name Edwina Clay. Didn't even query it."

"Let's hope the real Edwina doesn't notice the charges anytime soon," I said.

"She won't," Colt assured us. "It's a constructed identity. Hard to do, but possible. The guy I got it from worked for the government back in the day. Cyber security. Knows all the tricks."

"How come there's money, then?" I asked.

"I had to transfer credit through shell companies into the bank account to fund it. Shame we'll only get one-time use out of those lenses."

"Maybe not," Brooks said.

"What do you mean?" A prickle of unease tingled at the back of my neck. Brooks was planning something else, and I was sure I wouldn't like it.

"Not now. Let's get off the streets first." He turned to Clara. "You want to lead the way?"

"Sure." Clara started back toward the motel. "Follow me, boys."

# CHAPTER THIRTY-SEVEN

THE ROOM WAS AS EXPECTED. Two queen beds with garish comforters over them. A bathroom at the back, and a paper-thin panel on the wall that served as a television. We settled in and ate some snacks from our backpacks.

Brooks turned the TV on and flicked through the channels. To my relief, our faces weren't plastered all over the evening news. We took turns showering. There was a laundry room further down the block and Clara said she would wash our dirty clothes later that evening and repack them, ready for the road.

Once we were feeling fresh, Brooks got down to business. "I'm going to make some calls and hopefully get us new wheels."

"I'll make a resupply run," Colt said. "There must be a store somewhere close to here."

"I asked in the motel lobby," Clara said. "There's a super-market two blocks away. Walking distance."

"Good girl." Brooks motioned to Colt. "Take her with you. We can use Edwina Clay to purchase what we need."

So that was his plan. I shook my head. "Clara's done enough."

"Dammit, Hayden." Brooks turned on me with a scowl. "Don't make this harder than it needs to be."

"Then don't keep putting Clara in danger," I shot back.

"It's okay." Clara placed a hand on my arm. "I'll go with him. It's only a couple of blocks. How dangerous can it be?"

"At some point, our luck will run out," I said. "What if those contacts have worn off already? What if you're not Edwina Clay anymore?"

"They won't have worn off yet." Colt sounded sure of himself. "We have at least another couple of hours before her body rejects the altered DNA."

"Fine," I said, but I wasn't happy about it.

"Don't worry. I'll be fine." Clara squeezed my arm.

"Ready to go?" Colt asked.

"Sure." Clara moved to the door and opened it. She was about to step through, but then she stiffened and retreated. "No! no, no, no. This isn't possible . . ."

"What?" I rushed past her. Peered out into the parking lot. I saw nothing.

"A crazy." Clara's eyes were wild. She backed further into the room. "There was a crazy in the parking lot hunched over a dead woman. He was eating her, pulling lumps of her flesh off with his mouth."

"You telling me you saw one of those zombie people from the other reality?" Brooks asked her. He joined me in the doorway.

"Yes. Out there across from the room," Clara replied. Her voice trembled when she spoke. "There's a truck parked across four bays at the back. He's right there, in front of it. You must see him."

"Clara, there's nothing here," I said, stepping outside. I walked toward the truck she had described, my gaze sweeping the parking lot. There were no crazies. No dead women. And why would there be? We weren't in that world anymore. This was a different place where monsters didn't exist, and people didn't turn into mindless killers. I returned to the hotel room.

"You saw it, right?" Clara was standing motionless, her eyes on the door. "When you went outside. Please tell me you saw it."

I shook my head. "There are no crazies in the parking lot."

"There must be." Clara rushed to the door and looked out. After a moment, she turned back to us, a look of disbelief on her face. "It's gone."

"Because it was never there," I said. This wasn't the first time she claimed to see a crazy in this world. My mind returned to the incident in the safe house. We all assumed she was having a nightmare and carried a part of it out with her when she woke up. A sleep-induced hallucination. But she hadn't been asleep today. A knot of dread twisted in my stomach. "Are you absolutely sure of what you saw?"

"Yes. A hundred percent. That crazy was as solid as you are. The thing looked right at me. Lifted its head up and returned my gaze. I swear."

"Okay. I'm sure you—"

"I didn't imagine it," Clara snapped. "You didn't believe me back in the safe house. Why won't you believe me now?"

My gut clenched. Something weird was happening, and I didn't like it. "It's not that I don't believe you. I'm sure you saw something. But I didn't. Nothing is there."

Clara backed away. Her bottom lip trembled. "What's happening to me?"

I looked at Brooks, hoping he could provide an explanation. After all, it was his technology that brought us here.

But he was no help. "Maybe she's overtired."

"Maybe." I didn't buy that, and I was sure Clara didn't either.

"I still have to go get those supplies," Colt said. "I think it might be best if I went on my own."

Brooks nodded. "I agree. Clara is in no state to help you."

"I have to go." Clara took a step toward the door, even though she didn't look like she wanted to move. "You need Edwina Clay."

"There are other ways," Colt said. He was at the door now.

"Like what?" Clara sniffed and took a deep breath.

"He knows what he's doing," Brooks said.

"Is he going to put himself in danger?" I asked.

"It's not totally safe," Colt said. "Let's leave it at that."

"Honestly, I'm fine now," Clara said. She had regained her composure, but I could see she was still shaken.

"I don't want to risk it," Brooks said. He motioned to Colt. "Go."

Colt stepped out into the parking lot, then turned back toward us. "If I don't come back, if I get caught, don't come looking for me. Get as far away from here as you can."

"We know the drill," Brooks said. He met Colt's gaze. "Good luck."

"Thanks." Colt turned and closed the door behind him, leaving the three of us alone in the room.

# CHAPTER THIRTY-EIGHT

COLT WAS GONE for two hours. Brooks took the opportunity to make some calls using a device that looked a little like an earbud. He said it was a burner phone. Apparently, the terminology hadn't changed in over a hundred years.

He stepped outside to make his calls, leaving me alone with Clara. She was still on edge and kept looking toward the door as if she expected a crazy to come bursting through at any moment.

I told her to lie down, close her eyes, but she wouldn't. Instead, she paced back and forth, full of nervous energy.

"What's happening to me?" She asked at length. "I've seen things that aren't there twice now."

"Maybe you imagined it," I said, although I didn't really believe that explanation. "We've been walking for two days straight ever since we lost the car. You must be exhausted."

"We're all exhausted. No one else is hallucinating."

This was true. I didn't have a good answer. Instead, I sat on the edge of the bed and motioned for her to join me.

Clara finally stopped pacing and sat down. I put my arm around her, let her head rest on my shoulder.

"It's going to be okay," I said.

"Is it?" Clara asked. "Because I don't think it will be ever again. Look at what's happened to us. We are stuck in a living hell. And to make matters worse, I'm seeing things that aren't there."

"We'll figure it out." The words sounded hollow even as I said them. How *exactly* were we going to figure it out? It wasn't like we could go online and Google the answer. But I didn't know what else to say.

Clara didn't press the issue. "If I have to be in hell, I'm glad it's with you," she said.

"Me too," I replied as Brooks reentered the room. I looked up at him. "Any luck?"

"It took some doing, but I've arranged new transportation. You don't want to know how much it cost."

"Honestly, I don't care. So long as we have wheels under us." I couldn't take another day of walking. "How do we get ahold of it?"

"We have to meet the man with the car later tonight."

"He's coming here?" I asked.

"No. I wasn't willing to give out our location. Too risky. He gave me coordinates. It's not far."

"When?" I didn't like the sound of this plan.

"Midnight."

Now the plan sounded even worse. "You sure that's wise?"

"No, but I don't have a better idea," Brooks said. "Do you?"

I didn't. "How are we going to do this?"

"We go together, me and you." Brooks took a seat at a small table near the window. He leaned on it with his elbows. "We'll be careful. Get there early. Scope the place out. Colt will stay here with Clara."

"Good." I didn't want her anywhere near the pickup, especially in light of her recent turn.

Brooks fell silent for a spell, lost inside his own head. He stared out of the window to a building across the street—a homeless shelter where men and women in drab clothing came and went, their faces etched with misery.

Clara stood and headed for the bathroom, splashed cold water on her face from the sink, then returned and curled up on the bed with her back to me.

After a while, Brooks rapped his knuckles on the table and stood, motioning for me to step outside with him.

I followed him out, casting a glance back toward the bed before I pulled the door closed behind me. Clara didn't move. Either she was asleep, or her mind was occupied with other things. Like the crazy she had seen eating a woman in the parking lot, even though neither one was there.

Brooks wasted no time in confronting me once we were out of Clara's earshot. "What's wrong with her?"

"I don't know," I replied, which was the truth. The first time she hallucinated back in the safe house, it was easy to chalk it up to a nightmare. Lucid dreaming. I could not attribute her latest episode to such a mundane explanation. Try as I might to write it off as nothing but her exhausted mind playing tricks, deep down I knew this was not the case. Something else was happening.

"You think she's okay to continue on tomorrow?"

"I don't think we have a choice." I looked out over the parking lot toward the truck, hoping to see evidence—any little scrap of proof—that would validate what she claimed to have witnessed. As expected, I saw none.

"Maybe it's some form of PTSD," Brooks mused.

"Possible," I replied. But I wasn't sure I believed that. Were we convincing ourselves of an explanation to make the situation more manageable? Maybe she *was* suffering from posttraumatic stress . . . God, I hoped that was the case because we stood a chance of fixing it . . . But what if this was something else entirely? What if she really had seen that crazy? Did that mean they were bleeding between dimensions into our world, or was it a sign of something worse? I had no answers.

"We'll have to keep an eye on her," Brooks said. "Can't risk her wigging out at an inopportune moment."

"I know."

"If she becomes a liability…" Brooks didn't finish the sentence.

"She won't become a liability." And even if she did, I wasn't going to let Brooks do anything to her. If he tried, he would find himself on the wrong end of one of those guns we had stashed up on the hillside.

"Make sure that she doesn't."

I didn't respond. There was nothing left to say. And besides, there was a figure coming toward us across the parking lot now. A man carrying two large bags, one slung over each shoulder. Colt had returned with the supplies.

# CHAPTER THIRTY-NINE

WE LEFT to meet the man who was bringing us the car at eleven that night. Brooks had looked up our destination and memorized the route from the motel. Now he led me through the dark and empty streets with confidence.

This town was nothing like Refuge City. It was old and full of buildings that might have been quaint if it weren't for the obvious pall of decay that hung over the streets like a shroud. Empty storefronts. Abandoned buildings. Shuttered businesses. Again, my mind wandered to a comparison with some of those mill towns I knew from my previous life. Places that had lost their industrial roots and fallen into a spiraling decline.

We reached the center of town and the bridge that spanned the river. An odor rose from the water, pungent and cloying, and even though I couldn't see the nature of what flowed beneath us as we crossed over, I knew the water must be ripe with pollutants like the stream in the forest.

We reached the other side. Brooks kept moving, walking fast. On the few occasions that we encountered another pedestrian, he kept his head low, and his collar turned up. Once in a while, a vehicle passed us by, painting us in the glow from its headlights. But no one stopped or challenged us. If the senator's underlings were searching for us in Happenstance, they were looking in the wrong place. Or maybe they figured we were sleeping, and they were doing the same. But that didn't mean we were safe. The last time we made a trip like this, it ended in betrayal and death. The last thing I wanted to do was walk into another trap.

Brooks must have been thinking the same thing. As we approached the pickup location—a derelict factory in what must once have been an industrial area on the outskirts of downtown—he stopped and turned to me. "We should proceed with caution."

"Agreed." It was a little past eleven thirty. There were no streetlamps here. The landscape was dark and foreboding. Our destination, a squat four-story building with two tall chimneys on one end, loomed ahead of us across a cracked and weed-choked parking lot. It reminded me of a scene from a gangster movie. "You could have picked somewhere a bit less clichéd."

"What, like a downtown coffee shop?" Brooks asked.

"No. But maybe somewhere better lit, like a gas station, would have been nice."

"That would be great if there were such a thing as gas stations anymore," Brooks said. "The cars are electric. Fossil fuels ran out decades ago. Plus, they weren't exactly helping things."

"You must still need to charge them."

"Nope. Solar paint. Nanoparticles in the car's shell extract energy directly from the sun's rays, however weak they are. One of the few good things to come out of rampant global warming."

"There is no sun," I said. "I've seen nothing but depressing cloud cover since the day you brought me to this world."

"Doesn't need direct sunlight. It can capture up to eighty

percent of available solar energy. No need for gas stations or charging ports." Brooks looked irritated. "But enough of this. We're getting off track."

I studied the building ahead of us and noted the wide-open bay leading into the interior, spanning at least two floors. Huge sliding doors that probably hadn't moved in years stood on each side. Whatever was made here, it must have been big. A steelworks, maybe? "You think we're the first to arrive?"

"That's what I'm hoping," Brooks said. He struck out toward the building at a fast pace, striding across the parking lot until we reached the enormous double doors.

Here he stopped again, caution getting the better of him. The interior was impossibly dark, but Brooks was ready. He removed a small flashlight from his pocket and switched it on, sweeping the beam into the cavernous interior.

We appeared to be alone.

He stepped across the threshold, his free hand falling to the small of his back, where I saw a slight but definite bulge. Handgun. I wondered why he hadn't offered me one, or at least let me know that he had it, but now was not the time to stop and ask questions.

"Looks clear," Brooks said in a low voice. "We got here first."

"Looks can be deceptive," I said, studying the surrounding darkness. The building was large, with plenty of places to hide. But that worked for us, as well as those we were here to meet. "We should find somewhere to conceal ourselves. I don't want a repeat of what happened in the Packing District."

"Goes without saying." Brooks was already moving away from the doors, his flashlight beam lancing through the gloom and picking out an object in the darkness. A hulking piece of machinery, rusting and dead.

The perfect hiding spot.

We moved behind it and climbed up off the floor between

two sections of the machine's apparatus. This gave us a good view out across the factory floor without leaving us exposed.

Brooks clicked off the flashlight. Darkness rushed in around us.

For a moment I was blinded, my eyes struggling to adjust, but then the outlines of the factory walls and other pieces of rotting machinery became visible to me. And something else. A faint glow came from beyond the opening through which we had entered. Growing steadily brighter.

Headlights.

"Here goes," Brooks whispered in my ear. "If it looks safe, I'll go down and make the exchange. You stay here out of sight and cover me."

"You want to give me that handgun you have pushed into your belt?" I whispered back.

"Noticed that, huh?"

"Yeah."

Brooks pulled the weapon out and handed it to me. It wasn't as high-tech as the rifles we had concealed in the woods, looking like every handgun I'd ever seen. It was heavy in my palm. "Anything special about this?"

"Pretty much your standard handgun," Brooks replied under his breath. "If things go south, point and pull the trigger."

"Sure thing," I replied. The factory was dark, and I doubted my ability to hit a hostile without harming Brooks. "Don't blame me if I shoot you by accident."

"You'll do fine. You're a crack shot."

I gave him a quizzical look.

A faint laugh broke his lips. "You don't recall it, but your body will. Muscle memory. Like when we were shooting that drone in the woods. Trust me."

"Yeah." I fell silent because the car was entering the factory now. Except it wasn't one vehicle. It was two.

They drove in one behind the other.

The first car came to a stop fifteen feet from the entrance. The second one circled around behind it and stopped with its headlights illuminating the space.

A man climbed out of the first car. He stepped away from it and looked around.

"You can come out now," he said in a loud voice. "I don't bite."

I exchanged a look with Brooks. Was the man bluffing because he assumed we would have gotten here first, or had he and his companion concealed themselves somewhere in the darkness outside and watched us enter?

"I'm taking a huge risk coming here to bring this vehicle. The least you could do is trust me," the man said. "I assure you my companion and I are unarmed."

Brooks placed a hand on my shoulder—a signal to stay where I was—then he climbed down from the machine and stepped out, showing himself. "Had to make sure."

"I can appreciate that," the man said. "We both need to watch our backs. Which is why the man you arrived here with should come out, too."

There it was. He wasn't bluffing. We hadn't been the first to arrive after all.

Brooks walked toward the car. "My companion stays where he is. Insurance. Let's get this over with."

The new arrival shook his head. "That doesn't work for me. I don't like unknowns. Bring him out here or the deal's off. And if he's got a gun, tell him to leave it behind."

Brooks came to a stop. He turned to look in my direction, waved for me to come out.

I considered concealing the gun in the small of my back as Brooks had done but decided against it. I climbed down and placed the gun on the ground before revealing myself.

"That's better." The man smiled. "Come closer, both of you."

"What about your companion?" Brooks asked, nodding toward the second vehicle. "Let's see him."

"A fair request." The man motioned to the car. The door opened. A second man stepped out and stood with his arms folded, watching us. "Good enough?"

Brooks nodded.

I joined him, and we moved closer.

"Let's do this," Brooks said when we were ten feet from the car. "I transferred the funds from an offshore account. My part is done. Check with your contacts back in Refuge City. They'll confirm it."

"Already have. The car is all yours." The man tossed Brooks a sleek black key fob.

Brooks lifted a hand and snatched it from the air.

The man stepped away from the vehicle and moved around it, heading for the second car. His companion climbed back in and waited for him, then steered the car toward the exit. As it drove between us and our vehicle, the car slowed, and the passenger window slid down.

The man looked up at us. "Apparently my bosses back in Refuge City like you."

"We've helped each other out on occasion," Brooks said.

The man nodded. "Which is why they asked me to relay a message before I leave."

"And what would that be?" Brooks asked.

"Get as far away from here as you can. Right now. People are coming."

"What people?" Brooks glanced toward me then back. "I thought we had a deal?"

"We did. And we fulfilled it. But it was made known to anyone who might be interested . . . The two of you . . . There's a bounty on your heads. Too much money to ignore."

"You've got to be kidding me." Brooks took a sharp breath and cursed. "You betrayed us."

"Yes. But we also gave you fair warning." The window was already rolling back up, the car inching forward. "Good luck."

# CHAPTER FORTY

"GET THE GUN," Brooks shouted as he turned and sprinted toward the car. "We have to get out of here."

I ran in the other direction and snatched the gun from where I'd left it behind the machinery. By the time I reappeared, Brooks was steering the car around in a wide circle. I pulled the door open and jumped in.

"Some great friends you have there," I growled. "They turned us in."

"They aren't my friends. They're mobsters. Underworld criminal types. You swim with sharks you have to expect to get bitten."

"And it never occurred to you this might happen?"

"It occurred to me. I figured it was an acceptable risk."

"Why were you even doing business with them in the first place?" I asked as we sped toward the doors. "Aren't we supposed to be the good guys?"

"Where do you think we got all the parts for that machine that you and Professor Morecambe built? The same machine we used to rescue you from that alternate reality."

"I don't know. My memory got erased, remember?"

"The black market. That's where." Brooks was driving the

car in manual mode, his foot pressed against whatever passed for an accelerator on this vehicle. We shot forward toward the exit, faster and faster. "Now buckle up, it's about to get real."

"Look out," I said as a sleek dark shape pulled across the opening. A black car that was hard to see in the darkness because its lights were off.

"I see it." Brooks didn't slow down. Instead, he kept going.

The car wasn't long enough to block the entire space, but there was another one approaching fast across the parking lot. Another moment and we would be cut off.

"They're trying to trap us in the building," I said.

"I know what they're doing. Brooks pushed the car to its limit. If there was a gasoline engine under the hood, it would be screaming by now. But we were still moving in disconcerting silence. I couldn't explain why, but it was unsettling.

The second car had almost closed the gap. Another few seconds and we would either have to swerve back inside the building or crash.

"It's going to be tight," Brooks said through clenched teeth.

I reached out and put a steadying hand on the dashboard as the car barreled forward toward the diminishing gap.

I was sure we weren't going to make it.

I held my breath. Prayed that this wasn't how I would die.

We reached the exit a second before our escape route was blocked. Brooks slipped past the first car. Swung the wheel hard right to avoid the second one.

There was a bump, a grating of metal on metal as we made contact. The car shuddered. But it was only a light brush, and then we were in the parking lot and speeding away.

"Holy crap," Brooks hollered, spinning the wheel and sending the car into a sickening high-speed turn toward the road. He was actually grinning. "Talk about threading a needle."

"For the love of God . . . drive!" I glanced back through

the rear window. The two black vehicles had swung around and were giving chase.

"Let's hope they didn't bring any friends," Brooks said as we reached the road and peeled out onto it.

"And that they didn't call the cops on us." The men in the black cars were clearly not law enforcement. I assumed they were government agents. Spooks. Whether they had requested the help of local law enforcement would depend on if they wanted to announce their presence, or ours, to the locals. Since the plan was, apparently, to eliminate me quietly before anyone knew I was back from the alternate dimension—which would raise questions certain people might not want to answer—I thought it was unlikely we would find a police roadblock waiting for us. That didn't mean there weren't more spooks waiting to intercept us if we broke loose of the factory. After all, we had already evaded their drones and escaped on foot once.

"We've got incoming," Brooks said, confirming my worst fears. "Two more cars, dead ahead."

I turned to face forward again. Our pursuers were already on the road behind us, and now I saw another pair of cars driving side-by-side along the road toward us.

On one side of us was a high chain-link fence surrounding another factory building. On the other was a wall at least six feet high. There was no sidewalk here because it was an industrial area.

We were trapped.

"We have nowhere to go," I said.

"I can see that." Brooks wasn't slowing down. If we stopped, we were dead regardless. Better to play chicken.

"I have an idea." The gun was still in my hand. I lowered the passenger side window.

"Whatever you're going to do, make it quick," Brooks said. "We're going to hit them head-on."

I didn't answer. Instead, I leaned out and pointed the gun

at one of the fast-approaching cars. Wind buffeted my hand, making it hard to aim.

I squeezed the trigger.

The gun bucked in my hand. It was quieter than I expected. Maybe there was a built-in suppressor.

The bullet smacked into the road somewhere in front of the car. My aim was off. I was trying to hit the front grill.

I fired again. This time my aim was true. I saw a spark as the bullet slammed home.

It wasn't enough to incapacitate the vehicle, but it made the driver think twice about his course of action. He slowed down while the car to his right shot ahead. This opened up a gap between them. It wasn't much, but it was enough.

"Good job," Brooks said. He was already flying along, but now he pushed the car even faster.

As we reached the rolling roadblock, Brooks sped past the first car and swerved around the second, pushing through the space that had opened up before the two vehicles could close it again.

There was nothing but open road ahead of us. But when I looked back again, the cars that had been ahead of us were turning around to give chase. Then there would be four cars, not two, behind us. I didn't know how many bullets the pistol in my hand still held, but it wouldn't be enough to take out four speeding vehicles. Which meant we wouldn't stand a chance.

# CHAPTER FORTY-ONE

"Hurry," I said, craning my neck to watch the two black vehicles we had evaded a moment before turning in the road behind us. In doing so, they caused a roadblock that forced our other pursuers to stop. "Get us on a side street and out of sight before they start after us again. We don't have much time."

"What do you think I'm trying to do?" Brooks swerved around a parked car and almost lost control. He fought to steer the vehicle back straight.

"Holy crap," I said, breathless. "At this rate, we'll kill ourselves and do the senator a favor."

"I'm doing my best," Brooks said.

The cars behind us were giving chase again now, picking up speed.

"Hold tight." Brooks slammed the wheel hard to the right and careened onto a side street.

The back tires struggled to maintain grip, then found purchase. The car righted itself and shot forward, pushing me back into the seat.

There was another intersection ahead. Brooks took the corner fast enough for the back end to fish tail.

This road was narrow, with buildings pushing in on both sides. I tensed, praying we wouldn't clip a wall and crash. Our pursuers were nowhere in sight. They hadn't reached the intersection yet.

Brooks glanced at me and grinned. "Doing okay over there?"

"Can you please focus on driving?" I asked him, bracing myself against the dash.

The first black car was turning now. Accelerating away from the intersection. The others followed in quick succession.

"We still have company," I said, breathless. "Coming fast."

"I've got this." Brooks swung the wheel again, turning right and doubling back toward the main road. But instead of rejoining our original route, he took a left onto a narrow access road, barely letting up on the speed. Ahead of us was a factory complex, the buildings standing in stark silhouette against the night sky. He circled around to the back of the closest of them and stopped, killing the headlights. Then he relaxed back in the driver's seat with a sigh. "Now we wait."

I was dubious that such an obvious ruse would work and expected to see the sleek, black government vehicles appear at any moment. But they didn't. As the minutes wore on, I realized we were in the clear. But Brooks kept us parked, hidden behind the building.

That suited me. With each passing minute, there was less chance that the government spooks would still be in the area. With any luck, they would assume we were still fleeing blindly and focus their attention on other areas of the city.

After ten minutes passed, I spoke up.

"We can't stay in the city tonight," I said. "It's too dangerous now."

"I agree." Brooks didn't look happy. "I figure we'll sit it out here for a while longer, to be safe, then pick the others up at the hotel and keep moving. It's a shame. I was looking forward to a good night of sleep in a real bed."

"Can't be helped." I realized the gun was still in my lap. I placed it on the center console, within easy reach if I needed it. "You should call Colt on that burner phone earpiece you were using earlier. Give him and Clara a heads up and tell them to be ready when we get back to the motel."

"Can't do that." Brooks shook his head. "Now that they know we're here, they'll be monitoring the comms bands, looking for us. If they isolate the signal from my earpiece, they'll be able to track us again."

"And we'll lead them right back to the motel."

"Yes." Brooks took the earpiece out of his pocket and opened the car door. He dropped it to the ground and crushed it under his heel. He got back in with a dour expression. "No one will trace our signal now."

"You could have turned it off," I said. The earpiece might have come in useful later.

"Doesn't work like that. Even powered off, the earpiece can be located if you know what to look for. I used it to phone my contacts in Refuge City. If the bad guys were listening to that call, it's probably compromised."

This was true, I realized. Even in my world, government agencies like the NSA could track cell phones that were turned off. They could even activate a device remotely and listen to the conversations of whoever was carrying it without them knowing. Technology was a liability when you were trying to stay out of sight. That led me to another thought. "The people you got this car from double-crossed us. How do we know they didn't plant a tracking device in it?"

"Because if they had, we'd be dead right now."

That was a good point, but it led to another question. "Had you considered that when you pulled in here to hide?"

"It crossed my mind," Brooks admitted.

"And yet you still stopped, putting us at risk of being trapped."

"What was the alternative?" Brooks was sitting with his

eyes closed and arms folded, no doubt trying to catch a moment's rest during our downtime. "Try to outrun them and risk leading those people right back to the others at the motel?"

"Speaking of which, we should get back there." I didn't want to leave Clara any longer than necessary. Her strange turn earlier in the evening had left me worried. I wanted to believe it was stress, but I couldn't shake the feeling something more was happening.

"I think we've given it long enough," Brooks said. He opened his eyes and sat up. Started the car. He eased forward around the building, driving slowly, and scanning our environment left and right.

We were alone, much to my relief.

The motel was less than two miles away. It only took a couple of minutes to drive there, even with Brooks choosing a roundabout route and weaving back and forth through side streets to ensure we weren't followed.

Colt was waiting at the door when we arrived back. The relief on his face was clear. "What took you guys so long?"

"Ran into a little trouble," Brooks said. "We won't be getting any more help from back east. There's an underworld bounty on our heads."

"Figures." Colt's lips were pressed into a tight line. "Let me guess, we can't stay here."

"There are government agents scouring the streets as we speak. At least four cars. They tried to intercept us."

"I bet there's more," I said.

"More than likely," Brooks agreed, hurrying past Colt into the motel room. "Which means we don't have much time. They don't know where we went, but they will not stop looking."

"What's going on?" Clara had been lying on the bed. She was sitting up now, bleary-eyed. "I was worried about you."

"I'll explain later," I said. I didn't know if she'd gotten any sleep, but I was happy that she was resting at least. "We need to pack up and leave."

"Right now?"

"Yes. There's no time to waste." I could imagine those shiny black vehicles tearing around the corner at any moment full of government agents hell-bent on killing us. Every second we weren't putting miles between us and the motel increased the risk of getting caught.

Clara swung her legs off the bed. She slipped on her shoes, grabbed her backpack. It took us less than ten minutes to load the car with our gear and the supplies Colt had secured in town. That left only one thing outstanding.

"The guns we left on the hillside," Colt said. "We're going to need those, especially when we get to the Arizona Cauldron."

"We'll stop and get them on the way out of town," Brooks said.

"Wait," Colt said as Brooks climbed in the car. He rushed back into the room and reappeared a moment later clutching the comforters from the beds and four pillows, which he threw on the backseat. When he caught me looking at him, he shrugged. "We paid for this room and we're not going to use it. Figured we might as well be comfortable on the road."

"That's what we're stooping to, now . . . stealing pillows?" I raised an eyebrow.

"We're wanted for blowing up a building and killing hundreds of people," Colt said. "I can't imagine that taking a few pillows is going to move the needle much."

"Except we're innocent," I pointed out. "We didn't bomb that building."

"That won't make a blind bit of difference if we get caught," Brooks said impatiently from the driver's seat. "If we live through this, I'll buy the motel some new pillows. Now get the hell inside the car, all of you. Let's go."

# CHAPTER FORTY-TWO

WE DROVE through what little remained of the night and into the next day. At the edge of town, Brooks pulled over and I ventured up onto the hillside to retrieve the two weapons we had stashed earlier. I didn't want to take the time. We were fugitives. Government agents had almost caught and killed us once that night, and I didn't want to give them a second opportunity. But Brooks was adamant that we needed the guns, and he was right. If we ended up in a tight spot with only one handgun between us, we would almost certainly be doomed.

I put the weapons in the trunk and we pressed on. The landscape of this world was at times familiar, but different more often than not. Climate change had wreaked havoc upon the land and rendered all but what remained of the East Coast practically uninhabitable. Or so Brooks told us.

Brooks, Colt, and I took turns driving, although mostly the car was driving itself and we were passengers waiting to take over the controls should it become necessary. We did not include Clara in this duty because of what had happened in the hotel room. We couldn't risk her having another hallucination while she was in the driver's seat, even if there was little to do except watch the dashboard.

During the remaining hours of the night, we discussed our options and concluded it was not safe to stop before we reached the Arizona Cauldron more than sixteen hundred miles away. By that time, we should be safe from our pursuers, or so we hoped. This suited me. I was worried about Clara, and Darwin was never far from my thoughts. Every hour we delayed was another hour he spent trapped in a collapsing world. I didn't know if there was an answer waiting at the end of our trip, but the quicker we got there, the sooner we would find out.

An hour after we left Happenstance, with Brooks at the wheel, we passed near Pittsburgh, which lay to the north. I couldn't see the city because we gave it a wide berth out of an abundance of caution, but I couldn't help wondering what it looked like. I had visited Pittsburgh on a couple of occasions back in the other reality. Would this city look familiar to me, or would it be more like the sprawling and alien metropolis Brooks and his men had brought me to less than forty-eight hours before? I would probably never know.

As the night wore on, Clara slept. We had made a cocoon of sorts across the back seat, out of the comforters and pillows that Colt had liberated from the hotel room. She lay curled up in a fetal position with a pillow under her head. I propped one of the other pillows behind my own head and dozed for a while until it was my turn to watch the car drive itself. Even over a hundred years in the future, it was hard to allow a vehicle complete autonomy, even if that meant doing nothing but stare at the controls.

As dawn broke, we made our first pit stop. While we were eager to push on, we still needed to stretch our legs and take bathroom breaks. We pulled over on a lonely back road surrounded by the overgrown fields of what must once been a large farm. A barn was sinking into the ground, its timbers old and rotten, the roof sagging in the middle as gravity took its toll.

Standing apart from this was an old farmhouse that had burned at some point. Now it was nothing more than a blackened, roofless shell with empty windows that stared out like dead eye sockets. It reminded me of another place we had visited recently. Clara stirred beside me and must have thought the same thing.

"This looks like that farm where we met Clay."

"It does," I agreed. We met Clay Norton during our journey from Vermont to New Haven after we saw smoke rising from a farmhouse that had burned. In his mid-fifties, he looked like he had been born outdoors. Rough around the edges and hardheaded, he didn't hesitate to put a bullet between the eyes of a crazy, although he called them zombies, which I found to be a little clichéd. He was also a bit of a conspiracy theorist and thought the government had caused the world to go haywire by provoking the Chinese, or maybe the North Koreans, into releasing a deadly virus. In a way, he was right. Except that the government that caused the mess was in a different reality and the virus was a glitch in the process that created the world we had inhabited.

"Do you think he's still alive?" Clara asked.

"I don't know." When we parted ways with Clay, he was heading for Canada, which he was convinced had been spared. I wondered if her question was as much about Darwin as it was about the man who shared a meal with us on that farm and gave us his pistol. "I hope he is."

"If we ever get back there, we should look for him. He was nice."

"That's a tall order," I said. "Even if he made it all the way to Canada, he never told us his final destination. It's a big place."

"I guess so." Clara pushed the comforter away. She opened the car's back door, climbed out. "I'm going to take care of business."

# CHAPTER FORTY-THREE

WHILE CLARA HEADED behind the burned farmhouse to answer the call of nature, the rest of us stepped into a field on the other side of the road to do our business.

Afterward, I leaned on the car and waited for Clara to return. After so many hours cooped up, it was a relief to stretch my legs. Brooks and Colt took a stroll down the road to loosen their stiff muscles and returned a few minutes later.

Clara hadn't yet returned.

Brooks glanced toward the farmhouse. "She's been gone a while."

"Probably taking care of woman stuff," I said.

Brooks observed me for a moment, then went to the trunk and opened it, removing a bottle of water, which he made quick work of. After a couple more minutes, he brought the subject up again. "This is taking too long. I don't enjoy sitting here out in the open."

"We haven't seen a drone since the woods outside Happenstance," I said. "And there's barely any other traffic on this road. I think we're safe right now."

"I'd still rather be moving. Maybe you should go check on her."

Brooks had a point. Clara had been gone for a long time. She was probably fine, but now a nagging doubt hovered at the back of my mind.

"I'll go see where she is," I said and started across the barren field toward the charred and abandoned farmhouse. "Wait," Brooks called after me. He returned to the trunk and pulled out one of the rifles. "Take this."

"Don't you think that's overkill?" I looked around us. "We're in the middle of nowhere."

"Better safe than sorry."

I nodded and took the gun. There was no point in arguing, and I had to admit, the weapon gave me more confidence.

The farmhouse stood back fifty feet from the road. An overgrown driveway ran from a broken-down gate to the front of the building. I followed this and then circled around.

When I reached the back, I almost bumped into Clara, who was coming the other way.

"Hayden." She looked at the gun, then at me. "What are you doing?"

"Looking for you."

"Well, now you've found me." Clara started back toward the car.

"Everything okay?" I asked, sensing that something was off. I studied our surroundings but saw nothing unexpected.

"Yes. Everything's fine." There was a definite edge to Clara's voice.

I didn't believe her. "You're holding something back. What is it?"

"It's nothing . . ." Her voice trailed off. She stopped and turned back to me. Her eyes glistened.

"Tell me what happened." I closed the gap between us and put my hand on her shoulder.

Clara hesitated as if she was trying to decide what to say.

When she spoke, I could hear the stress in her voice. "I saw another one."

"A crazy?" An icy chill enveloped me.

"Yes. I looked up, and it was out in the fields, coming toward me. I was going to scream, almost did, but when I blinked, it wasn't there anymore. Vanished."

"You must still be tired," I said, but even I didn't believe the words. This was more than a waking dream, exhaustion, or some weird form of PTSD. This was trouble. Something was not right, and it scared me.

It obviously scared her, too. She looked into my eyes. "What's happening to me?"

"I don't know."

"I've had two hallucinations in the last twelve hours. Whatever is happening to me, it's getting worse."

"We don't know that." I hoped I wasn't kidding myself.

"Trust me," Clara said. "It was different this time."

"What do you mean?" I asked.

"I'm not sure how to explain it." Clara frowned. "You know that feeling when you first wake up, and you're half out of the dream, but not quite?"

"U-huh." I glanced back toward the car. Brooks and Colt were waiting there, watching us. Brooks looked impatient.

"Well, it was like that, only not quite. It was like I was here, but also somewhere else, both at the same time. I felt . . ." Clara stopped and searched for the right word. "Unmoored."

I didn't know how to respond. Whatever was happening to Clara was outside the realm of my knowledge. Maybe she was suffering from some unique form of posttraumatic stress related to our journey through the other world, or perhaps she was experiencing something entirely different. I thought about Emily and how she had turned into a crazy right in front of us. How I'd been forced to shoot her before she killed Darwin. It was the single worst moment of my life. What if Clara was heading toward a similar fate? What if she was on the verge of becoming one of those mindless, violent creatures? Would I have the stomach to kill her as I had Emily? I didn't want to know the answer. In the end, I decided there was nothing I could do. If Clara was on the verge of becoming a crazy, there was nothing I could do to stop it. In the meantime, I chose to believe that it was nothing so dire. Exhaustion. Stress. Anything that could give me hope.

Clara was looking at me, waiting for a response. I slung the rifle over my shoulder and nodded toward the car. "I'm sure it's nothing to worry about."

Clara folded her arms. "Promise me something."

"What?"

"If I change, if I become one of those..." She stopped and took a trembling breath. "If I go like Emily, I want you to take care of it."

"Clara..."

"I'm serious. I want you to do it. Not Brooks. Not Colt." Clara fixed me with a stern gaze. "It has to be you."

"You can't ask me to do that," I said because I wasn't sure I could.

"I'm not asking. I'm telling you."

"Why would you want me to—"

Clara cut me off. "Because if I go crazy, like Walter and Emily, I want the last thing I see to be the face of someone I love."

I was rendered momentarily speechless. "You're saying that you—"

"Don't make a big deal of it. I had to tell you how I feel. That's all." With that, she turned and strode back toward the car, leaving me staring at her back.

# CHAPTER FORTY-FOUR

I DIDN'T MENTION Clara's latest hallucination to the others. I didn't wish to alarm them, but more than that, I was aware that they might view her as a liability. I did not believe she was turning into one of those mindless crazies that inhabited the other world. Something else was going on. I was convinced of this . . . but needed time to process my hunch and make sense of it. Even though I wasn't sure exactly what was causing the hallucinations. I only hoped the condition would not grow worse in the meantime.

We continued on with Brooks in the driver's seat for the first six hours. After this, Colt took a turn. Then, as the day wore on, I slipped into the captain's chair, so to speak.

Being in charge of a true self-driving car was a bit like watching paint dry. Without the need to pay attention, I struggled to stay awake even though I had slept on and off for a couple of hours already.

Colt was in the passenger seat next to me, while Brooks took my former position in the back and rested with a pillow behind his head. After a while, I heard soft snores and when I looked in the rearview mirror, he was asleep. If I hoped for a conversation with Colt, I was out of luck. He too had given in to the Sandman and sat slumped with his head against the passenger door window.

To my surprise, Clara was not sleeping.

"How long do you think it will take us to reach Lake Tahoe?" She asked.

"If we drive straight through, a couple more days," I told her. "Of course, that depends on how easy it is to get through the Arizona Cauldron."

"What do you think we'll find when we get there?"

"Lake Tahoe?"

"No. The Arizona Cauldron. It sounds awful, judging by what we've been told."

"I guess we'll find out soon enough," I said. We had already passed south of Chicago and, a little while later, north of St. Louis. The trip was made longer because we were sticking to back roads. I figured we were about halfway to the Arizona Cauldron and already we appeared to be in a no-man's-land. The middle of the country was a vast and empty wasteland dotted with abandoned reminders of a world long gone. Climate change had done everything the people of my world predicted it would, and more. A starving population fighting over the scraps of what remained had done the rest. It was no wonder the government had come up with a way to ease the problem. If only they had done a better job of it, maybe Clara and I would still be content in the alternate reality Vermont instead of fleeing for our lives.

"What if we can't find this woman, Professor Morecambe?" Clara asked. "Or what if we find her and she can't help us?"

"I don't know," I said. This had been on my mind, too. We stood little chance of clearing our names if we couldn't prove that the alternate realities were collapsing. Even then, there was no guarantee that we would be successful. Our enemies were powerful people with resources we could only dream of. Our situation was dire, but we had no choice but to press on.

For the next few hours, Clara was silent. Colt relieved me at the wheel, and I switched places with him. I sat in the passenger seat and stared out across the landscape. When we pulled over to stretch our legs and do our business, we also took the time to eat a light dinner cobbled together from the supplies that Colt had gathered in Happenstance.

We ate surrounded by what must once have been wheat and corn fields but was now parched and empty land starved of water by a drought that Brooks told us had lasted for more than a quarter of a decade. An unthinkable amount of time. I could see a heavy layer of dust that lay across the fields. A house and two barns that stood next to the road. The dust had drifted up against the sides of the structures in a way that reminded me of sand dunes. Further away, silhouetted against the cloud-laden sky, stood an aging water tower that had lost most of its cladding and leaned at a precipitous angle.

It looked to me like black-and-white photos I had seen that were taken during the Great Depression when the Plains States suffered the devastating natural disaster known as the dust bowl. I wondered what would happen to all of that dust if the wind picked up. Not long after we got back on the road, I found out.

# CHAPTER FORTY-FIVE

THE STORM HIT EARLY in the evening as we were approaching Kansas City. Brooks was behind the wheel again while I occupied the back seat, along with Clara.

"Looks like we've got trouble," he said, slowing the car and then bringing it to a stop.

I leaned forward and stared through the gap between the seats at the landscape ahead of us. An angry black cloud stretched across the horizon, billowing out, and folding upon itself as its advanced.

Clara pushed up next to me and let out a gasp. "What is that?"

"Dust storm," Brooks said. "Big one."

"Is that normal?" I watched the towering wall of dust moving toward us like a landlocked tsunami, reaching so high into the sky that it appeared to merge with the sky above and become one with the dirty gray firmament.

"They happen from time to time, but I was hoping we would avoid running into one." Brooks sounded alarmed. He was already turning the car around. "It's still a long way off, probably five or ten miles, but it's coming fast. We have to find shelter."

"Can't we sit here and ride out the storm?" Clara asked, peering through the car's rear window as we raced away from it.

"Sure," Colt replied. "If you want to end up stranded out here in the middle of nowhere afterward."

"If that storm reaches us and we're out in the open, we'll get sandblasted. The winds inside the monster are probably howling at eighty miles an hour or more." Brooks chimed in. "It will strip the paint right off the car."

"Without solar paint, we'll have no power to keep going once the batteries drain down," Colt said. "And we won't be getting our hands on another vehicle anytime soon, all the way out here."

"We'll still have enough juice to get us to Kansas City, though, right?" I asked.

"Probably." Brooks was speeding away as fast as he could, but the storm was gaining on us. "The batteries will get us several hundred miles, even if we're not able to recharge."

That was a relief. "If worse comes to worst, we can always find another vehicle in Kansas City," I said. "Or at least get this one repaired."

"Not going to happen." Colt turned to look at me. "KC is all but a ghost town. The city has been scoured by years of extreme weather. Dust storms. Tornadoes. Lightning strikes."

"What's left of downtown is nothing but a maze of ruined buildings," Brooks said. "The city was evacuated more than fifty years ago."

"None of that matters," said Colt. "The dust will do worse than strip our paint. It will get in every crevice, destroy wiring, seize moving parts. We'll be lucky to drive another mile, let alone all the way to Kansas City and beyond."

"What about the abandoned farm where we stopped to eat?" I asked. "Can we make it back there?"

"Your guess is as good as mine," Brooks said. "But it's our

best chance of finding somewhere to shelter and ride the storm out."

"Probably our only chance," Colt said. He twisted around in the front seat to look back at the approaching storm, then glanced at Brooks. "You might want to punch up the speed a bit, or we might not make it."

"I'm going as fast as I dare," Brooks said. "We wreck the car and it's game over."

"I don't like this." Clara's hand slipped into mine.

The barren landscape was whizzing past us on each side, but we were still losing the race. Behind us, the dust storm gobbled up everything in its path like a hungry predator. I now realized why the fields were so barren and empty. How could anything grow out here with such extreme weather? "How many miles away is that farmhouse?" I asked, hoping it was nearer than I thought it was.

Brooks confirmed my worst suspicions. "At least ten. Maybe fifteen."

"Can we make it that far?" Clara watched the storm bearing down upon us with wide eyes. "It's getting so close."

"I guess we'll find out soon," Brooks said. "Keep your fingers crossed."

We would need more than that, I thought. Fingers, toes, and maybe even a few prayers to any deity who would listen. Getting stuck out here without a vehicle would be a death sentence. Even if we could walk all the way to Kansas City hoping to find a new car—an idea Brooks had already shot down—we would risk encountering another storm. And if the dust could strip paint from a car, imagine what it would do to an exposed human?

I tried not to think about that, and instead stayed silent as Brooks pushed the car to the limit. He was driving in manual mode now, and muttering curses under his breath with each glance in the rearview mirror.

After a while, the farmhouse and barns appeared ahead of

us like an oasis of salvation. Assuming we could reach them and find somewhere to shelter. But the storm was done playing with us. As we covered the last mile of cracked and baked asphalt, the storm's leading-edge finally caught up and rolled over us like a wave, blotting out what was left of the late evening light, and threatening to leave us lost in a blinding swirl of dust.

"It's now or never," Colt said through gritted teeth. "Get us to that farmhouse."

"What you think I've been trying to do?" Brooks retorted.

The dust was getting thicker now. The farm was nothing more than a pale silhouette up ahead. Another few minutes and we would lose sight of it entirely. But that was the least of our problems. The wind howled. It buffeted the car and threatened to send it veering wildly off the road.

Brooks cursed again, louder this time, as he struggled to maintain control.

The storm had us in its grip now. Our surroundings were reduced to a dark, and featureless void filled with dust. An incandescent aura enveloped the car, fed by strange blue sparks that danced across the vehicle's outer shell. It would have been beautiful if it were not so terrifying.

"What is that?" Clara asked in a small voice. She shifted closer to me.

"It's the dust," Brooks said, "moving so fast that it's inter-acting with the car's alloy surfaces."

"And taking the paint off at the same time," Colt said gravely. "I hate to say this, but I think we're done for."

# CHAPTER FORTY-SIX

"I AGREE." Brooks was losing his battle to keep the car on the road. But it wasn't only the intense crosswinds howling inside the storm that rocked and pushed at the car. It was the dust, which was so thick it reduced our visibility to little more than a few feet. "I can't see for shit."

"Maybe we should stop before we kill ourselves," Clara said.

"If we do, we will never start again." Brooks gripped the wheel so hard that his knuckles were white. I could see his arm muscles bulging as he fought to keep us moving in a straight line. Even so, the car's nose drifted and sent us bumping into the unpaved dirt at the side of the road until he could regain control.

"We must be getting close to that farm by now," I said, peering out into the churning gloom for any sign of the two barns and the abandoned house. But it was useless. I had seen snowstorms in Vermont, blizzards that turned the landscape into a void of white nothingness, but I had never encountered a lack of visibility this complete.

"For all I know, we've driven right past it already," Brooks replied. The car took another jolt sideways, and he grimaced, swinging the wheel with all his might until we found hard asphalt under us again.

I watched the luminescent blue sparks flickering across the car's body with a growing sense of alarm. Each tiny point of light was more paint being eaten away, which meant the vehicle would produce less solar energy to keep us going.

A bolt of lightning lanced out of the blackness and smacked into the earth so close to us I could almost feel the electricity.

Clara screamed.

"Just when I thought this couldn't get any worse," Colt complained above the melee.

"All those dust particles rubbing up against each other at such high speeds are causing a buildup of static electricity. Tons of it." Brooks was hunched over, peering through the windshield as if getting closer to it would somehow allow him to gain extra visibility. "It's going to get worse before it gets better."

As if to prove him right, another bolt slammed down right in front of us with a resounding boom, sending pieces of asphalt flying and creating a small smoking crater in the road.

Brooks swerved to avoid this new obstacle.

Gravity pushed me sideways into Clara.

I sat back up and took deep breaths, trying to calm my racing heart.

"The car." When Brooks spoke, his voice was ragged. "It must be attracting the lightning. We're lucky we haven't sustained a direct hit."

Up ahead of us, another fork of lightning lanced down, but this time it wasn't looking for the car. It was too far away. But in that brief flash, I saw a faint outline emerge through the choking dust. The unmistakable shape of a building.

"There. On the right," I said, slapping the back of the driver's seat. "It must be the farm."

"I see it," Brooks said.

"Hurry it up, we can't take much more of this." Colt was stiff in his seat, staring out into the swirling void. "Get us out of this hell."

"What do you think I'm trying to do?" Brooks snapped back.

We were close now. The buildings emerged out of the dust like ghosts. Gray specters against the heaving storm.

Brooks swerved off the road without slowing down and onto a narrow trail leading to the farm. We bounced and bumped over deep ruts and jutting rocks. The house came into focus ahead of us, but he ignored it and drove on past, heading for the barns.

"Hang on to something, this is going to get rough," Brooks shouted and swung the wheel to the right.

Clara let out a small whimper and grabbed a handle hanging from the roof of the car above the door.

I braced myself against the front seat.

The barn sat directly in our path. The double doors were standing cracked open, but not wide enough. Not by a long shot. I wondered how sturdy they were, and if it was a good idea to be ramming them at high speed. But it was too late to do anything else.

As the car smashed into the doors, sending splintered wood flying in all directions, I took Clara's hand in mine and squeezed.

# CHAPTER FORTY-SEVEN

WE BURST through the doors and into the barn, shards of broken wood flying everywhere. Instinctively, I turned away and closed my eyes, fearing the windshield would not hold and we would be peppered with splinters. But we weren't.

Once we were far enough into the barn to avoid the dust blowing through the hole we just made, Brooks slammed on the brakes, which engaged the car's automatic emergency system, and we skidded to a halt. The abrupt stop sent Clara and me sliding forward in our seats, but the seatbelts tensed and held us back.

The sudden calmness around the car was eerie. We could still hear the wind howling like a banshee outside, and dust was billowing in through the hole we had created in the barn doors, but other than that, everything was calm. Except for an electronic voice that kept repeating the phrase 'collision detected. Exit the vehicle if safe to do so.'

"How do I turn that damn voice off," Colt said, stabbing a finger at the touchscreen dashboard in irritation. Whatever he did worked. The voice abruptly stopped mid-sentence. "That's more like it."

"We'd better get out and inspect the damage," Brooks said.

As if in answer, the touchscreen flickered, blinked a couple of times, and went dead. The car's interior lighting soon followed suit.

"That can't be good," Clara said. She unclipped her seatbelt and opened her door.

"I've got a bad feeling about this." Brooks was already climbing out of the car.

I did the same, happy to be out of the vehicle after the wild ride through the storm.

The car was in a sorry state. When we took possession of it in the abandoned factory in Happenstance, it was painted a gleaming white. Now there was very little of that paint left. The car's body was a dull silver color. I reached out and touched the metal. The surface was rough under my fingers. The dust had done as Brooks predicted it would.

Colt was already at the front of the car, fighting to open the crumpled hood. After a minute, he won the battle and stared into the engine compartment for a moment. Then he swore. "Hate to say this, but we're not going anywhere anytime soon."

"Is it bad?" Brooks was already heading toward him.

"Dust got in here. Half the circuit boards are shorted."

"Can you fix it?" Brooks asked.

Colt shrugged. "I can try, but not without the right tools."

I stepped away from the car and explored our surroundings. The barn was large. The front half was an open space while the back half was divided into stalls that lined the side walls, leaving the middle open. I could see a second set of doors at the other end. I assumed they must've kept horses here at some point. There were certainly no tools anywhere, and I said as much.

Brooks nodded in defeat. He glanced toward the splintered barn doors, hanging askew on their hinges, and the dust that was blowing in through the gap our car had made. "Maybe after the storm passes, we'll find what we need in the other barn or inside the house."

"We'd better," Colt said. "Or it's going to be a long walk out of here."

"Let's worry about that when the time comes," Brooks replied. He went to the trunk, opened it, and started pulling out our gear. "In the meantime, we should make ourselves comfortable. We're going to be stuck in here for a while."

# CHAPTER FORTY-EIGHT

WE UNLOADED the car and built a small fire for warmth and light at the back of the barn between the stalls. To make sure we didn't burn down the building with us inside, Colt used his hands to scoop out a pit from the earthen floor. We pulled boards from the interior walls and broke them up into smaller pieces for firewood. The timber was tinder-dry thanks to the unyielding drought that Brooks said had enveloped this area for years. The downside was that it also burned quickly, and the fire required constant feeding.

It had been three hours since we found shelter and the storm was still howling outside, with no sign of letting up. The wind still blew dust through the busted barn doors, but thankfully it couldn't reach us so far inside the barn. I almost asked Brooks how long these dust storms usually lasted, but I didn't. I might not like the answer. And even when the storm did finally blow past, there was still the question of our car, which appeared to have suffered a catastrophic electrical failure. If we couldn't get it back on the road, it wouldn't matter how long the storm lasted.

The conversation was sporadic as we ate a supper cooked over the open flames. None of us were in any mood for idle chat. Eventually, after the fire burned down, we retreated to a pair of stalls where our sleeping bags were now set up. Clara and I took a stall on one side of the barn while Brooks and Colt slept on the other. The darkness was smothering with only a flashlight to illuminate our surroundings. Clara didn't want to be alone, even if I was only a few feet away, so we zipped our sleeping bags together. She lay in my arms with her head against my shoulder. I turned out the flashlight to conserve power and closed my eyes.

Sleep was elusive for both of us.

After a while, Clara spoke in a low voice. "Do you think life will ever be normal again?"

"I'm not sure," I replied. Ever since that gas station in Vermont, we had been running from one enemy or another. First, it was the crazies. Then it was the monsters. Now it was a government obsessed with killing us. We were caught in a no-win situation. We couldn't make a life on this world because of a situation I didn't even remember, yet if we returned to the world I viewed as my home, we would surely die. That reality was falling apart. If there was a third option, I could not see it.

"I meant what I said earlier," Clara whispered. "If I'm turning into one of those mindless people . . . If I go like Emily…"

"We'll worry about that if it happens." I didn't believe she was turning into a crazy, but I did think there was something else at work, which worried me as much. I lay in silence for a few moments, processing our earlier conversation. "About the other thing that you said earlier . . ."

"Yes?"

"I love you, too."

Clara drew a sharp breath in the darkness. Her hand grazed my cheek. "I'm so relieved. I wasn't sure you felt the same way."

"Why would you think that?"

"I don't know . . . because . . ." She trembled, and I realized she was crying.

"Hey." I stroked the small of her back with my hand, kissed the top of her head. "I didn't mean to upset you."

"You didn't. I wasn't expecting . . ." Clara took a deep breath. "It's been a tough couple of days, that's all."

"I understand." I stared up into the darkness and listened to the wind and dust howling beyond the thin walls of the barn. "I wanted to tell you, in case . . ."

"I know." There was movement as Clara wiped the tears from her eyes.

After that, we fell silent. I tried to fall asleep but couldn't. I kept thinking about our destination, further away than ever. Would we find Professor Morecambe there? A woman I had apparently recruited to our cause but of whom I had no recollection. I sat up, reached for my pants, slipped out the small flat slip of metal Brooks had given me back at the safe house. The strange credit card shaped object with a small lens at the top that the professor had left with him. The message on this device had started our whole journey. Come to Fahrenheit, it had told me. I wondered what lay in store for us there, and if we really could rebuild the dimension hopping machine and rescue Darwin. Then I thought about Clara, and her strange hallucinations. Maybe an answer to those lay in the mysterious place called Fahrenheit, too.

I turned the silver device over in my hand, held it up to my face to see if I could activate it again. Receive another message that would tell me we weren't wasting our time travelling across the country like this. But the device remained stubbornly dead. Was Morecambe dead too? If so, our last hope would be gone. But there was only one way to find out. Reach our destination and see.

I yawned and slipped the device back into my pocket, then settled down into the sleeping bag. I was asleep within minutes this time.

# CHAPTER FORTY-NINE

I AWOKE IN THE DARKNESS. Something had disturbed me, but what? Clara was still lying next to me, snoring softly, with one arm draped across my chest. It wasn't her. I lay there in the cubicle and wondered if whatever had roused me from sleep would repeat. Then a sudden thought occurred. Had they found us?

I fought back a rising sea of panic. It would be so easy to kill us as we lay there, vulnerable. The guns were still in the car's trunk. Now I wished we had possessed the forethought to take them out and keep them close. It was a stupid mistake. We had been too wrapped up in dealing with the sandstorm and our damaged vehicle. Plus, the guns were right there if we needed them, safely locked away a few feet from where we now slept.

None of that did any good if soldiers were even now creeping into the barn to kill us. An image of men wearing night vision goggles and camo flitted through my mind.

I moved Clara's arm from my chest, sat up, and peered off into the darkness, praying that I wouldn't see the telltale beam of a laser sight or the dim outline of a special forces operative standing in the stall entrance.

For a moment, the barn was still, then a faint sound reached my ears. Like the shuffling of feet on a dirt floor. It was a brief disturbance, barely more than a second or two. But this must be what had woken me.

I held my breath and strained to pick up the sound again, pinpoint from which direction it had come. But everything was silent again now.

"What's going on?" Clara stirred next to me.

"Don't know," I whispered. "Thought I heard something, that's all."

I heard her draw a sharp intake of breath. "You think we've been found?"

"There's one way to know," I said, pushing myself out of the sleeping bag and standing up. I picked up the flashlight. "I'll go look around."

"No." There was panic in Clara's voice. "What if there's someone out there?"

"Then we're better off knowing before they find us cornered in the stalls," I whispered. Again, I thought of the guns, so close, yet they might as well have been on the moon for all the good they did us at that moment. But maybe I could get to the car and retrieve one of them from the trunk. That way, we would stand a fighting chance if we really had been discovered. I looked in Clara's general direction, resisting the urge to turn the flashlight on right there and announce our location to any hostile operatives that might be in the barn. "I'm going out there. Stay here and stay quiet. Don't follow me."

"I really don't like this."

"I know." I wasn't exactly looking forward to stepping out of the stall, but what choice was there?

I padded to the door and eased it open, praying that the hinges would not squeak. Thankfully, they didn't, despite their years of neglect.

The barn beyond the door was silent and black. I stood for

a moment at the threshold waiting for any would-be attackers to reveal themselves. When no assault came, I clicked the flashlight on. The beam illuminated the narrow swath of floor ahead of me. I swung it around, picking out the other stalls, our vehicle, and the damaged doors we had burst through earlier in our haste to get out of the storm.

Then I realized something.

It actually was silent. And I could see no dust blowing in anymore through those wrecked barn doors. The storm must have passed.

This much, at least, was a relief. But I quickly realized that it also meant we were vulnerable. While the dust was swirling at a hundred miles an hour and lightning bolts were slamming into the ground outside, it was unlikely anyone would venture near the barn. Now, though, the calmness that had rushed in behind the tempest provided an opportunity for any would-be attackers.

Not that I saw anyone.

I stepped out of the stall and made for the car. When I reached it, I lifted the trunk and found one of the rifles we had used to shoot down the drone in the forest. The weapon gave me an instant surge of confidence.

I closed the trunk again and kept moving.

My finger hovered over the trigger. I was tense as a coiled spring.

Upon reaching the barn doors, I stopped. They were hanging off their broken hinges at an angle, their leading edges splintered and broken. Beyond this, through the gap our car had made, I saw a flat and barren landscape stretching off into the darkness, broken only by the thin asphalt strip of the road we had been journeying upon before the storm blocked our path. And I saw something else too. The solitary figure of a man standing out near the road, oblivious to my presence.

# CHAPTER FIFTY

I FROZE in the doorway and raised the gun.

The man stood with his back to me, presenting an easy target. He appeared to be alone, and I could see no visible means of transportation.

"Turn around slowly and identify yourself," I said. "And so you know, I am armed."

For a moment the man didn't move, then he turned to face me, and I saw that this was no stranger. It was Colt.

"Whoa. Easy there. Don't shoot me, OK?" he said, walking back toward me.

"You gave me quite a scare. I thought we'd been discovered." I lowered the rifle. "What are you doing out here?"

"Call of nature." Colt pushed his hands into his pockets as he walked. "I noticed the storm had passed and figured it was better to come out here than do my business in the barn. Didn't mean to wake you."

"It's fine." I looked around at our surroundings. The storm had left everything coated in a thick layer of rust-colored dust. It swept up the sides of the barn and blew across the road, making it hard to distinguish where the fields ended, and asphalt began. The night was eerie in its calmness.

"Well, I'm heading back to my sleeping bag." Colt side-stepped me and made for the barn. "You coming?"

"Sure." I took one last look around and followed him back inside.

As we passed the car, Colt stopped. He opened the trunk and took out the other rifle.

"Just to be safe," he said, checking to make sure the weapon was loaded. Then he turned and continued on toward the stall he was sharing with Brooks.

I followed a short distance behind him. Once he entered the stall and pulled the door closed, I returned to my own sleeping bag, where Clara was sitting up waiting.

"Everything okay out there?" She asked.

"It was Colt taking a leak." I kneeled down, set the gun on the ground next to the two sleeping bags we zipped together earlier, and crawled inside. "Everything's fine."

"Then what's with the gun?" Clara waited for me to settle down and snuggled next to me. "You expecting trouble?"

"Only a precaution," I told her. "If the senator and her people really had found us, they would have caught us unawares. I don't want that to happen."

"God, I hate this world."

"Me too." If the world hadn't gone to hell, I would have been back in my apartment in Burlington by now and working on my second book while I dreamed of the literary success I would achieve with the first. Brooks told me I was the leader of a group whose purpose was to fight the corrupt government of this world and expose their lies. He said I had a whole other life. People in this reality who relied upon me. I didn't remember any of that, and I wasn't sure that I wanted to. The world I remembered was a far cry from this desolate and ravaged place full of danger and despair. The life I remembered was ordinary. Normal. I wanted that back. But then again, if the reality I thought was my own hadn't glitched and started to collapse at the very moment I pulled into that gas station, I would never have gotten to know Clara. I would have paid for my gas and driven off without giving her a second thought. So maybe one good thing had come from all of this.

Clara yawned and mumbled a quick good night.

I whispered my reply in her ear, then held her close and closed my eyes. Neither of us spoke again, and soon I could tell she had fallen back asleep. I tried to do the same, but my mind wouldn't shut off and I lay awake in the darkness. When I eventually did drift off, I dreamed of Colt standing out by the road, flanked by a pair of those creatures from the other reality. And as they bore down upon me, and ripped me limb from limb, I heard him laugh.

# CHAPTER FIFTY-ONE

When we awoke the next morning, Colt and Brooks were already up and working on the car. I went to see how they were getting on while Clara busied herself making breakfast for us all.

Upon my approach, Brooks looked up from the open engine compartment. "If you're in a good mood, you won't be for long."

I fought back my frustration. "That bad, huh?"

"Put it this way," Brooks replied. "If we don't find a whole workshop full of tools in that farmhouse yonder and enough spare parts to build a new power plant for this car from scratch, we might as well settle down and homestead right here."

"That's beyond bad." I peered inside the engine compartment but saw nothing I recognized. A bunch of metal plates that resembled etched circuit boards, a square box constructed of a material I couldn't identify, and what two glass cylinders, one on each side of the box, containing some kind of liquid or gel. The various components were connected by thin filaments I assumed were wires. Brooks had called this a power plant and not an engine, but to me, it looked like neither.

"Tell me about it," Colt said in a dry voice. "Damned dust got in here. It wrecked the circuit boards and shorted the wiring. If only we'd found shelter sooner, we might have been okay."

"Too late for that now," Brooks said, stepping back and slamming the hood.

"I'll go check the farmhouse and the other barn," Colt said, starting toward the barn doors. "I don't hold much hope, but I need to do something."

"Clara is making food," I called after him. "Why don't you come and eat first and then we'll all go together and see what we can find."

"I guess." Colt turned back toward us. "Even if we do find what we need, we still can't charge the batteries. So much of the solar paint is missing."

"Let's deal with one problem at a time, shall we?" Brooks wiped his hands on his trousers and took a step toward the rear of the barn, where I had left Clara. Then he stopped dead in his tracks as a low rumble shook the barn.

It came from above us. And it was getting louder.

"What the hell is that?" Colt asked, looking up even though there was nothing to see but rafters and joists in the gloom above us.

"Trouble. That's what it is." Brooks turned back toward the car. The rifle colt had taken from the trunk in the early hours was leaning against a wooden post. Brooks scooped it up. "Where's the other one?"

"Back in the stall." I turned and sprinted toward the back of the barn, but Clara was already heading toward me with the rifle in her hand.

"I think we've got company," she said.

"Tell me about it." I took the rifle from her and together we made our way back to Brooks and Colt.

"Anyone have any ideas?" I asked, hoping for a miracle.

The rumble had changed to a high-pitched whine. Dust

blew in through the barn doors and billowed in the air. Something large was landing out on the road. Maybe even more than one something.

"If I did, I'd have told you about it already," Brooks said.

"What about those other doors at the back of the barn?" Clara asked, glancing over her shoulder. "We could go out that way."

"And do what?" Colt shook his head. "There isn't even any cover out there. We'd be sitting ducks."

"Better than staying here and waiting to get shot."

"I have no intention of doing that," Brooks said. He hoisted the gun and started toward the front of the barn. "If I have to go, I'm going down fighting."

"Looks like it's time for a good old-fashioned shoot-out." Colt reached for the gun that was in my hands.

I backed up out of his reach. "No offense, but I'm keeping this."

"Four of us and two rifles," Colt grumbled. "I knew I should've gotten more."

"There's the pistol," I said.

"Guess that will have to do." Colt reached into the car and grabbed the handgun.

"And I'll grab a big stick and wave it around, shall I?" Clara's sarcasm would have been amusing if we weren't in such a dire situation.

"I'd rather you went back into one of those stalls where it's safe," I said to her.

"Really?" Clara was not amused. "And how long will that stay safe?"

"I don't think anywhere in this barn is safe right now," Brooks said. He was standing to the side of the doors and peeked out, careful not to reveal himself. "It's worse than I thought."

"Gunship?" Colt asked.

"Two of them. And a transport. Just landed."

"Shit. I wonder how many troops are inside that thing?"

"We're about to find out. The transport's back hatch is open. There will be soldiers coming our way any moment." Brooks pulled his head back and stood with his back flat against the barn wall. He held the gun tight to his chest, ready to bring it around and shoot the first attacker through the barn doors. "I hate to say it guys, but I think this is the end of the road."

# CHAPTER FIFTY-TWO

WE WERE GOING to come under attack at any moment. And this time, I was certain, we would not get out of it alive. That didn't mean we should give up without a fight.

Clara refused to retreat to one of the old horse stalls and take shelter, so I took her hand and led her over to the car. We kneeled behind it. It might not be any good as a getaway car, but it would provide some meager cover when the barn doors burst open and the soldiers who were undoubtedly disembarking those gunships and the transport vessel outside came bursting through.

I leaned the gun on the car's hood and aimed it at the front of the barn. Colt, armed only with a pistol, took up a position opposite Brooks on the other side of the barn doors.

Then we waited.

For an eternity nothing happened. I could hear the whine of the gunships' engines as they idled, but no one appeared in the gap between the doors, and from my vantage point, I couldn't see anyone outside, either.

I looked at Brooks.

He shrugged.

"What are they waiting for?" Colt said in a low voice. "If we're going to shoot at each other, I'd like to get it over with."

"Apparently, they don't feel the same way." Brooks looked like he was going to risk another peek outside the barn, but then thought better of it and stayed where he was.

"Maybe they're surrounding the barn before they attack to make sure we don't sneak out through some other entrance," I said.

"If they are, they're taking their sweet time." Brooks cradled his rifle, one finger hovering over the trigger. "This is the slowest tactical assault I've ever seen."

"Guess we wait and see what happens," Colt said.

As it turned out, we didn't have much longer to wait.

A voice drifted into the barn. I recognized it immediately as Senator Kane.

"Jason?" She said in a loud voice, referencing Brooks by his first name. "Hayden?"

I exchanged another glance with Brooks. He motioned for us to stay silent.

The senator waited a moment to see if we would reply, then spoke again. "I know you're in there. I want to talk. Nothing else."

Considering what had happened back in the Packing District before we fled the city, I didn't believe a word of it. Neither, apparently, did anyone else.

Brooks hitched the gun higher in his arms and answered her. "Sorry, Senator, but I find that hard to swallow. Now, why don't you tell me what you really want?"

"Jason. I swear, I'm here to talk. I'm unarmed."

"And the soldiers you brought with you?" Brooks replied. "Are they unarmed as well?"

"I have some soldiers me, for my own protection. But they won't shoot, I promise."

"Like that creature you set upon us in the warehouse didn't bite, huh?"

"That was unfortunate, but I didn't have any choice. If you come out and meet me, I'll explain."

"I don't think so."

"What about you, Hayden?" The senator called out. "You don't have your old memories, so you aren't encumbered by prejudice the way Brooks apparently is. You're also smart. There would be troops in there right now executing all of you if I gave the order. You know that. Think about it."

Brooks motioned for me to stay silent. I was happy to oblige.

The senator tried again. "I really don't have time for this. I'm taking an enormous risk in coming here. If I wanted you dead, you already would be. I don't want to see you all dead. I'm not the enemy. How can I prove that to you?"

Now I spoke up. "You can start by climbing back into whatever brought you here and leaving along with those soldiers you have out there. All of them."

"And then what?" The senator didn't sound like she was going to leave. "You sit in that barn with a broken car a thousand miles from civilization until you starve to death or get shredded by another dust storm?"

"Maybe."

"This is ridiculous." The senator fell silent for a moment. I wondered if she was conversing with her troops. Strategizing. When she spoke again, it was not what I expected. "All right, then. If you won't come out here, then I'm going to come in there. I'm approaching the doors now. I'm alone. I would appreciate it if you didn't shoot me the moment I enter."

"It's tempting," Brooks retorted with a wan smile.

"And it would also be foolhardy," the senator replied. "I've instructed my men to hold their fire and await further instructions. But if they hear so much as a single gunshot, they are under orders to raze the barn to the ground."

"I doubt they would do that," I said. "They'd be killing you, too."

"Ah, but they wouldn't, would they? There's only one person you would want to shoot at. Which means I would already be dead."

I couldn't fault her logic. "Okay. Come on in. We won't shoot so long as you are alone and unarmed, as you claim."

"That's very magnanimous of you," the senator said. She appeared in the doorway, hesitated a moment to make sure we weren't lying, and then stepped over the threshold. She looked at Brooks, then Colt, before her gaze settled on me and Clara. "Good. you're all here. Now, let's get down to business."

# CHAPTER FIFTY-THREE

BROOKS STEPPED AWAY from the door and gave Senator Kane a wary eye. "What do you want, Belinda?"

It surprised me to hear Brooks refer to the Senator by her first name. I wondered if it was to telegraph how little respect he had left for her as a powerful politician.

The Senator didn't flinch. She looked at the guns pointed in her direction. "Do you think you could lower those before we chat?"

Brooks hesitated, then lowered his weapon. I did the same. Colt pushed his pistol into the waistband of his trousers.

"That's better." The senator moved further into the room.

I wondered what her entourage outside thought of this brazen display of confidence that we wouldn't shoot her on sight. After all, she had betrayed us once and a lot of people were dead because of it.

"Would you mind answering my question now?" Brooks said. "What's with the sudden show of friendliness?"

"I was always your friend, Jason," the senator replied. "You know that."

"Friends don't usually set you up to be eaten by a monster from another dimension," Brooks said with cool detachment.

"You tried to kill us. It really wasn't very nice. I'm resisting the urge to return the favor."

"We've already covered this ground." The senator projected an aura of outward calm that I was sure must be a front. "As I've already said, the incident back in Refuge City was unfortunate. But it was necessary to ensure my safety. You need a friend in Congress, and I wouldn't be much good to you with a bullet in my head."

Brooks didn't look convinced. "No one is going to kill a sitting senator."

"Not so that it can be traced back to anyone in power. But trust me when I say that the stakes truly were life or death."

"I know," Brooks said coldly. "I watched my men get slaughtered. I saw the aftermath of that bomb that you placed in our building."

"Don't be so naïve. That bomb was nothing to do with me. I wasn't even aware they were planning to go that far. I'm sorry some of your men died. Really, I am. And they would've lured you to that warehouse whether or not I was there. The end result would have been the same."

"You didn't have to go along with it. I trusted you."

"I know. I broke that trust. But I had to convince certain people much more powerful than myself that *they* could trust me. That I was not a liability. It was the only way to make sure I could be useful to you and One World in the future."

"You could at least have warned us it was a trap."

"And then you wouldn't have come." The senator gave a weary sigh. "Look, what's done is done. The powers that be trust me again, or at least they have decided that I'm too dangerous to dispose of at the current time. I still have access to information. Not as much as I had before they discovered I was working with you, but some. Eventually, they may decide that I'm back in the fold for good and slacken my leash. Until that time, the best I can do is help you out of the situation you currently find yourself in."

"Speaking of which, how *did* you find us?" I asked, step-ping out from behind the vehicle.

"How do you think?"

"The car. You were tracking it."

"Not me, per se. You played right into the hands of the Multiverse Project Committee when you contacted the crim-inal underworld to procure another vehicle."

"Guess you can't trust anyone these days," Brooks said. "Even lowlife criminals."

"Which you should have known all along." Senator Kane folded her arms. "But don't worry. I faked the tracking data to cover your tracks. The committee thinks you're heading in an entirely different direction. Only myself and my men know your real location."

"Am I supposed to be grateful for that?" Brooks asked.

"You should be. Getting that car was a huge risk."

"I had no choice. The drones you sent after us took care of our first car. It wasn't like we could go rent something."

"The drones were nothing to do with me. You brought that upon yourselves by not checking Hayden for tracking devices the minute you brought him back from that other world. You're getting slack, Jason."

"Maybe I am." Brooks shrugged. "Why don't you get to the point."

"Good idea. I bought us some time. Made sure the tracking information from your vehicle got lost on its way to the committee. Computer glitch. But that won't fool them for long. More gunships could be heading this way as we speak. Probably are."

"You mean like the ones already sitting outside with their weapons pointed at the barn?" Brooks asked.

"Yes. Exactly like those. Except the difference is that no one inside them will be in a talking mood." The senator glanced back toward the barn doors. "We don't have long, so I'll make this quick. One of those gunships out there is at your disposal, along with the pilots. I don't know where you intend to go, but they will take you there."

"Just like that?" Brooks didn't look convinced.

"Yes. The pilots can be trusted, I assure you. They are both sympathetic to your cause, as are the rest of the men out there."

"I find that hard to believe."

"Nonetheless, it's true. I have spent the last several years quietly recruiting people whom I deemed could be useful including members of the military at various levels. Call it paranoia if you want, but I believed it was prudent to have allies should the need ever arise." The senator paused for a moment. "Now it has."

I wanted to make sure I understood what was being offered to us. "You're giving us a gunship and its pilots, who will fly us anywhere we want. You will then take that other gunship and the transport and leave."

"That about sums it up." The senator nodded.

"How do we know your gunship won't turn around and fly us all the way back to Refuge City to be turned over to the authorities?"

"You don't. You will have to trust me."

"A tall order given your recent track record," Brooks said.

"Look, there will be more gunships here at any moment. It might be thirty minutes, or it might be four hours, but they will come. And if you are still here when they do, you will die. No one is looking to arrest you or drag you back to Refuge City. Hayden isn't even supposed to be in this world anymore. This barn will become your tomb. By the time anyone stumbles across your remains, all that will be left of you will be bleached and unidentifiable bones scattered across the dusty fields. Take my offer or leave it. Your choice."

There was a moment of silence as each of us contemplated this. Clara touched my arm, passing a silent message to me. When I looked at Brooks, he gave a slight nod.

Like it or not, the senator was our only way out of this.

"I guess we have no choice but to trust you," I said to the senator. "We'll take the gunship."

"Good." The senator's lips creased into a slight smile. Then she turned and walked back toward the barn door. "I'm leaving now, and I suggest you do the same before someone less friendly than myself shows up."

# CHAPTER FIFTY-FOUR

THE SENATOR WAS ALREADY CLIMBING into her personal transport by the time we gathered our belongings and exited the barn. She walked up the ramp without so much as a backward glance and disappeared inside. A minute later, the ramp closed, and the transport vessel rose into the sky amid a cloud of choking dust. One of the gunships followed behind.

The Senator had not lied to us. There were no soldiers waiting to mow us down. No creatures from the alternate dimension straining against their handler's leashes to leap at us. Instead, a solitary gunship waited with its hatch open and two pilots sitting in the cockpit. And what a gunship it was. It looked like a cross between a helicopter and a fighter jet, except there were no rotor blades or wings. Instead, a pair of nacelles sat snug to the aircraft's fuselage, one on each side, within which the engines sat. I could see thrusters lining the underbody of the vehicle, no doubt for vertical lift. Cannons were mounted above the engines. A larger twin-barreled cannon was slung underneath the cockpit, while a fourth gun covered the aircraft's rear. The entire thing was painted a dull battleship gray. A set of metal stairs led up to the hatch nestled in front of the right nacelle.

"Guess we're not traveling first class then," Colt said as we approached the vehicle.

"Who cares?" Brooks said as we reached the stairs. "I'd rather take my chances flying in this one than wait for more of them to arrive piloted by less friendly individuals."

"Can we get out of here?" Clara said, pushing past us and starting up the stairs.

I almost told her to hang back, because I didn't trust the senator, but then I thought better of it. If this was part of some elaborate trap, we were going to walk into it at some point, anyway. Might as well be now.

I followed her up and ducked through the hatch, finding myself in a cramped and narrow space behind the cockpit. There were eight jump seats pressed flat to the fuselage, four on each side of the center aisle. I lowered one and helped Clara strap herself in before doing the same. Brooks and Colt took seats opposite us while one of the pilots retracted the stairs and closed the hatch.

Once the cabin was secure, he turned to us. "The senator told us to take you wherever you wish."

Brooks looked at me. "You want to tell him?"

I really didn't. I couldn't shake the feeling that this was a bad idea, although perhaps not as bad as sitting around to be massacred by special forces troops who worked for a corrupt government that had labeled us as terrorists. My hand dropped to my side, and the small metal card in my pocket. The one Professor Morecambe had given to Brooks. Come to Fahrenheit, the professor's message had said. When I asked what that was, Brooks had told me it was an outpost on Lake Tahoe. I figured Tahoe was good enough. If we could get that far, we could find our own way from there. I relayed this to the pilots.

"Tahoe's a mighty big place with not much near it." The man hesitated. "Any specific location?"

I exchanged a look with Brooks. Enough to tell him I didn't trust these people with our final destination.

He overruled me.

"Fahrenheit." Brooks gaze never wavered from me.

"Really?" The pilot exchanged a glance with his colleague in the cockpit. "Fahrenheit. You sure about that?"

"Quite sure," Brooks replied.

The pilot shrugged. "Whatever. Your funeral."

To me, by way of explanation, Brooks said, "I'm done with beating around the bush. We trust these people, or we don't. Either way, I want this over with."

"Your call," I told him, hoping that Brooks knew what he was doing. "How long will it take to get there?"

"A few hours," the pilot responded from the front. "You might as well settle down and relax."

A couple of hours sounded far better to me than the days-long drive we were facing before we encountered the dust storm. I wished we hadn't told the pilots our final destination, which would have provided a level of protection if this all turned out to be a cunning subterfuge, but what was done, was done. At least it brought us closer to finding Darwin. And as the senator had already pointed out, if she wanted us dead, she could have done so there and then in the barn instead of providing us with a ride. I told myself it was fine, and hoped I was right.

The second pilot had retaken his seat. He spent a moment checking his instruments, which were displayed on a touch-screen similar to the one in the car we were leaving behind in the barn. Then he exchanged a look with his colleague.

I sensed a shift in the atmosphere within the cabin. Something was wrong. It didn't take long to find out what.

"Better hold on to something. We need to beat a hasty exit," the first pilot said.

"Trouble?" Brooks asked.

"You could say that," the pilot replied. "We have incoming. More gunships. Two of them. Ten clicks out."

"With any luck, they haven't noticed us yet," the other pilot said.

"I wouldn't count on it," his colleague replied. "I think it's time we left."

# CHAPTER FIFTY-FIVE

OUR GUNSHIP ROSE into the air so fast that my stomach lurched. Thrusters rumbled beneath us, causing the entire thing to shake like it was about to come apart. I didn't know who built these military vehicles, but they were nowhere near as smooth or comfortable as the car we were leaving behind.

When I had recovered my equilibrium, I glanced out of a small cabin window set into the fuselage near my head. I saw the barn below us, and the rest of the farm buildings lining the dust-covered and empty road. Apparently, very few people ventured this far into America's heartland, and I could see why. From our new vantage point high above the ground, it became clear how desolate and ravaged our surroundings were. I didn't know how often dust storms occurred, but they must have happened frequently enough to render what was once arable land uninhabitable. I could see the remains of other buildings further away. Another farmhouse and more barns, in the same deplorable condition as the one within which we had sought shelter, or maybe worse. What looked like a row of grain silos had lost much of their former shape and were now nothing more than wrecked shells with twisted and mangled metal panels clinging to buckled structural supports. I wondered if the high winds within the dust storms had torn them apart.

There probably wasn't a living soul for hundreds of miles in any direction. And we hadn't even reached the Arizona Cauldron yet. A place Brooks described as a true hellscape, with temperatures that reached higher than those in Death Valley, and water was impossible to find. I was happy to be flying over it instead of driving through it.

"Better hold on," the lead pilot said from his seat on the left side of the cockpit. "I'm going to punch out of here before those other gunships arrive. I'd rather not pick a fight with men I've probably shared a mess hall with."

"You really think they'd fire on you?" Brooks asked.

"They will if they think you people are on board," the pilot replied. "We'll be labeled as traitors. They'll shoot us down in a heartbeat for colluding with terrorists."

"How would they even know we're aboard?" I asked.

"Heat signatures." The second pilot glanced back into the cabin. "We aren't supposed to be carrying troops, which means there should only be two of us aboard."

"Not to mention that we shouldn't be here, either. The senator was supposed to be heading for Toronto on a diplomatic trip with us and the other gunship as her escorts. That was her cover story. We turned off our positioning systems and went dark before taking a detour to rescue you."

"And we're grateful for that," Brooks said.

"Don't mention it," the first pilot replied. "Now grab on to something. Here we go. It's going to get loud."

The pilots fell silent and turned back to the job at hand.

The rumble from the thrusters abruptly cut off and for a split second there was silence in the cabin, but then the side engines roared to life, screaming to a high-pitched crescendo. I took the pilot's advice and grabbed a metal handle above the window next to the jump seat. A moment later, we shot forward, accelerating so fast that I was pushed back into the seat. I struggled to breathe. It was like someone had placed a hundred-pound block on my chest.

In the seat behind me, Clara groaned.

I held on for dear life.

Across the aisle, I heard Brooks let out a grunt.

Then, almost as quickly as it came upon us, the incredible pressure dropped to a manageable level. I breathed a sigh of relief and took another glance out of the window. The barn within which we had sheltered, and the surrounding farm, were nowhere in sight now. I didn't know how far we had traveled during our brief burst of extreme speed, but it must have been many tens of miles.

"Sorry about that," a voice said from the cockpit. "The rest of the trip will be smoother, I promise."

"I hope so," grumbled Brooks. "It's a good thing we never had time for breakfast, or it would be all over the floor by now."

"That was some ride there for a minute," Colt said with a grin. "Better than any roller coaster."

"Or worse, depending upon your point of view," I told him.

"Not a fan of roller coasters, huh?"

"Not so much." My single roller coaster experience had ended in disaster many years before when I was a senior in high school. I lost the corn dog I had consumed less than thirty minutes before. My date, who was the captain of the school cheerleading squad, didn't give me a second date. Or a goodnight kiss, for that matter. I drove home with bits of corn dog still stuck to my shirt and a memory that would shape my interaction with carnivals and state fairs from that moment on.

Of course, the memory wasn't real. It was part of an implanted back story provided by the same people who were now trying to kill me because I had the nerve to come back from the alternate reality they dumped me in. I wondered briefly why they would bother giving me such a detailed and embarrassing memory. Did they do this with everyone they sent over, or were they just trying to humiliate me?

"Hayden?" Clara broke my train of thought.

Her voice sounded strained.

I twisted in my seat to look at her. "Everything okay?"

"I'm not sure." Clara rubbed her temples. "I feel so strange. Lightheaded. It's like I'm here, but I'm not."

"Probably the effects of extreme acceleration," Brooks said.

"Maybe." Clara's face drained of color. Her eyes looked sunken in. There were dark rings around them.

"Did you have another hallucination?" I unclipped my lap belt and turned to face her.

Clara shook her head. "No. Nothing like that. It's... I don't know... Brooks is probably right. The acceleration affected me." She forced a weak smile. "I'll be all right."

"You sure about that?"

Clara nodded. She took a deep breath. "Yes. I'll be fine. I need a few minutes is all."

"All right, then." I turned frontward again and re-clipped my lap belt. I wasn't convinced that the gunship's sudden acceleration had left her feeling untethered and lightheaded. Brooks didn't know about the turn Clara had taken behind the farmhouse when we stopped for a bathroom break. We had kept that from him because I didn't want Clara to be viewed as a liability. Something else was going on, I was sure of it. The question was, what?

# CHAPTER FIFTY-SIX

WE FLEW for another ninety minutes, while below us, increasingly hostile terrain unfolded. I gazed from my window to distract myself from thoughts of Clara and the strange ailment that afflicted her. I had no answers. No way to help her. All I could hope was that the solution would present itself because I could not bear the thought of losing her.

The Arizona Cauldron didn't look like much from above. I had flown out West many times, visiting California and Nevada over the last several years. A vacation with my brother in Los Angeles, and several trips to Las Vegas, although I was not a heavy gambler. I liked the energy of the city. On those tedious and too long flights from the East Coast, I had gazed down upon the mountains and canyons as we tracked across the Western states.

The wrinkled and hard-baked landscape, painted in earth tones broken only by the occasional river or shimmering Lake might as well have been the surface of Mars for all the signs of civilization it possessed. The Arizona Cauldron looked no different. It was unremarkable in its blandness, at least from the air. I suspected, however, that it would be a different story if we had been forced to cross through it by land. I saw no cities, no signs of life. The only nod to mankind was the occasional glimpse of a thin asphalt ribbon winding through the parched valleys.

My first glimpse of Lake Tahoe came as we approached from the east. The pilots had dropped altitude. We skimmed a thousand feet above the mountain peaks and circled around, looking for a suitable place to land. I had never visited Tahoe before but had seen plenty of photographs. It was the largest Alpine Lake in the United States. It drew tourists in the thousands to play on its glistening blue surface. At least in my reality. In this world, the lake was reduced to a mostly dry bowl with a much smaller amount of water clinging to existence in the center. The settlements around the old rim—villages that had served summer tourists frolicking on its waters and skiers in the winter months—appeared as ghost towns when we flew over them. The buildings were obviously abandoned. Broken roads empty of traffic added to the eerie feeling of desolation.

I wondered what we would find at Fahrenheit, the destination Brooks had given to the pilots. One of the men had questioned him, which struck me as odd. Your funeral, he had responded. Now, as we drew close, a twist of dread coiled in the pit of my stomach. What were we getting ourselves into?

It wouldn't be long before I found out.

The pilots found a place to land on the cracked and dry lakebed a mile from our destination. This spot had been selected so that we wouldn't be easily observed.

When the gunship had come to rest, I unclipped my lap belt and stood up, retrieving my backpack from under the seat and slinging it over one shoulder. I picked up the gun and hitched it over the other.

The pilot who ushered us into the gunship back at the barn left the cockpit and opened the hatch before lowering the stairs. I waited for Brooks and Colt to disembark and then let Clara go ahead of me.

The heat smacked me in the face the moment I stepped

from the gunship. It was like walking into a blast furnace. It was no wonder the lake had all but dried up. I looked out across the lakebed toward the former shoreline that must once have been covered in forests of fur and pine trees but was now mostly decimated with only the hardiest of specimens clinging to life.

"This is where we say goodbye," the pilot said, standing in the hatch. "I don't know what you expect to find here, but good luck."

I watched the pilot retract the stairs and close the hatch. Moments later, the thrusters fired, and the gunship rose into the cobalt blue sky, soon to be lost in the glare of the unrelenting sun. Once again, we were on our own.

"Might as well get moving," Brooks said, looking toward the cluster of buildings sitting at the old shoreline that must surely be Fahrenheit. "The quicker we find Morecambe, the sooner we can clear our names."

"And find Darwin," I said, glancing at Clara.

But she didn't respond. She was staring off into the distance with a glazed expression.

"Hey, you alright there?" I asked, placing my hand on her shoulder.

For a moment, she didn't respond. Then she looked toward me, startled. "We can't stay here. The crazies are coming."

"What the hell is she talking about?" Brooks turned to face us.

"I don't know," I answered, then turned my attention back to Clara. "There are no crazies here. We're safe."

"That's because you can't see them." Clara took a step backward. "But they're coming."

"Okay. We don't have time for this." Brooks looked nervous. "Is she okay to walk?"

"Your guess is as good as mine." I was worried about Clara. Whatever was happening to her must be speeding up. I studied her face. Her eyes moved from left to right, tracking something that the rest of us could not see. I touched her arm and repeated to her the question Brooks had asked me. "Are you okay to walk?"

Again, she was slow to respond, then her roving eyes snapped around to look at me, and the fear on her face turned to one of puzzlement. It was obvious she had not been listening. "What did you say?"

"We need to leave. Get to Fahrenheit. Can you walk alright?"

"Yes."

"Good," Brooks said, impatient, and started walking toward the old shore. "Let's go."

"Wait," I called after him. We were both carrying large and possibly illegal guns. I wasn't sure it was a good idea to stroll through a town, even if it was a settlement clinging to the edge of existence, with rifles over our shoulders. "What about the guns?"

"Don't worry about it. No one will care, trust me." Then he continued on with Colt tagging along behind.

"Guess this isn't the Lake Tahoe from our world," I said to Clara as we followed behind.

But she didn't answer. She was too busy studying our surroundings as we walked, watching for phantoms that only she could see.

# CHAPTER FIFTY-SEVEN

FAHRENHEIT TURNED out to be the only inhabited place left on the lake. It had once been a thriving tourist destination known as Stateline that straddled the border between California and Nevada, with casinos on the Nevada side and none on the other, where commercial gambling was illegal. Now it was a rundown cluster of bedraggled buildings a stone's throw from extinction. The main street, which had once housed those casinos, restaurants, and hotels, looked nothing like a tourist trap now. It reminded me of an old Wild West movie set with wooden buildings of dubious construction interspersed between the derelict shells of the old gambling dens. Nothing here was high tech. I only saw a few vehicles. When we walked into town, the residents watched us with suspicion.

"Don't suppose you have a plan?" I asked Brooks as we neared the center of town.

"You're the one with the message from Professor Morecambe," he replied. "See if she sent you another one."

"I looked last night back at the barn. There was no message."

"We hadn't reached Fahrenheit yet. Look again."

"Not now. Let's get our bearings first," I said, unwilling to remove the metal credit card device out in the open until we knew it was safe. "I'm not sure—"

"We need to get off the street," Clara interrupted, her voice rising in pitch. She pressed close to me. "Right away. I don't like it out here. It's not safe."

"What's up with her now?" Brooks asked, irritated. "We can't afford for your girlfriend to lose it and draw attention. We're outsiders. A place like this…"

"We're also wanted on terrorism charges," Colt added. "Let's not forget that."

"Not an easy thing to forget," I said, then turned to Clara. "What do you see?"

"crazies. So many of them. All around us. They know we're here." She gave a half sob. "I see monsters too, slinking along the rooftops. They're everywhere."

"That doesn't make sense," Brooks said. "What she's seeing and describing… it sounds like the other reality where we found you. Those half-human creatures you call crazies can't be here. It's impossible. Realities don't interact with each other."

"Unless they're collapsing," I reminded him. "Isn't that what you told me was happening to my reality, that it was collapsing into another one?"

"Let me rephrase that. Artificially created realities don't merge with real ones, even if they are failing. There are no crazies or monsters here. None."

Clara disagreed. She lunged forward and gripped Brooks by his lapels. "You don't understand. They *are here*. I see them. If we don't get off the street, they will kill us all."

Brooks shook himself free. He glared at me. "You need to control her. She'll get us all killed, and not by crazies."

"I agree with one thing," said Colt. "We have to get off the streets and calm her down."

"Let's do it, then." People were looking our way. We might be on the other side of the country, but that didn't mean we were safe. All it took was one person to recognize us and make a call. "Any idea how?"

"Over there." Brooks pointed toward a ramshackle wooden building wedged between two taller brick ones. A hand-painted sign nailed above the door read Last Chance Tavern.

"Better than nothing." I took Clara's arm and steered her off the street. Her eyes were wide. They darted from side to side. She mumbled under her breath, but I couldn't make out what she was saying. Her grip on reality was faltering. I sensed it, but I was powerless to do anything about it.

# CHAPTER FIFTY-EIGHT

THE TAVERN WAS DIMLY LIT and small. Odors of stale beer and fried food hung in the air, reminding me of dive bars I had frequented in my youth. We made our way to the back of the room and found a free table. Brooks slipped his rifle and backpack off and set them against the table, then went up to the bar for drinks, more to blend in than because we wanted them.

I removed my own backpack with some relief and dropped it next to the chair, then placed my rifle nearby before sitting down.

Clara was still studying her surroundings as if she expected a monster to leap out at any time and attack us, but at least she was silent now. It broke my heart to see her in this state, but I was powerless to do anything about it. At least until we found the enigmatic Professor Morecambe. Maybe she would have an answer.

Brooks soon returned carrying four glasses and deposited them on the table before taking a seat.

"Ball's in your court, Champ," he said to me. "Whatever you need to do next, you should do it now."

"I don't know what to do next," I admitted, removing the

credit card-sized device from my pocket. I held it in front of my face, as I had back in the safe house. Nothing happened. It remained blank. There were no new messages. I placed it on the table. "This thing isn't working, and if I'm supposed to do something now we're here, I don't know what it is. Had my memories wiped, remember?"

"Right you are." Brooks sighed. "I hope Morecambe had some plan in mind other than giving you a vague destination."

"Assuming she's still alive," Colt added.

"Yes. Assuming that." Brooks took a sip of his drink and winced. "Backwater swill. They probably make it in an old barrel behind the tavern."

I tasted the beer. "It's not so bad."

"Says the man with no memories."

"I still know how beer is supposed to taste. We did have it on my…" I stopped myself. "In the false reality."

"We're getting off track," Colt said. "About the professor…"

"I told you already, I don't know where to go from here," I said, a little more sharply than I intended. But my frustration was spilling over. After everything that happened, all the dangers and challenges we faced to get here, we ended up sitting at the back of a dive bar with no way to finish our journey. Worse, Clara appeared to have slipped into a state of semipermanent hallucination. She was with us in body, but I had no clue where her mind was. She stared off into the gloomy corners of the room and acted like she saw horrors lurking there that remained invisible to the rest of us.

"Maybe we should find somewhere to shelter for the night," Brooks said, "since no obvious course of action has presented itself."

"Better than sitting here for the rest of the day," I said. Other patrons were casting suspicious glances our way. Some carried handguns on their belts. A few had larger weapons. They talked in hushed tones and watched us over their beer glasses. Clara's obvious distress didn't help matters. "You know any good hotels in these parts?"

"Funny." Brooks glanced toward the bar. "You know what they say. If you need a straight answer, ask the bartender."

The bartender was a burly individual with more tattoos than blank skin. An intricate spider's web design covered his shaved head. His short-sleeved shirt was tight enough to leave no doubt regarding his muscular build. He prowled behind the bar like a caged tiger and looked as friendly as a porcupine.

"You really want to do that?" I asked.

"No. You got a better idea?"

"I wish."

"That's what I thought." Brooks pushed his chair back.

My gaze shifted to the tavern door, where another man now stood. He was almost as muscle-bound as the bartender, but without the tattoos. A heavy leather jacket hung on his wide frame despite the heat outside. He surveyed the bar with a quick head movement, then started in our direction. "Forget about the bartender. We have a problem."

Brooks glanced toward the door and stopped, half out of his seat. "This doesn't look good."

"I think it's time we leave," Colt said, rising.

"Stay right where you are," the man said. He moved with surprising agility, given his weight. He reached the table before any of us could react and fixed me with an unblinking stare. "I've been waiting for you."

"We're not looking for trouble," I said, ready to reach for the rifle if the need arose.

"Neither am I," replied the man. "Come with me. Quickly."

"That's a hell of a request considering we haven't even been introduced yet," Brooks said. "Who are you?"

The man mumbled something under his breath that I

didn't catch, but was probably a curse word. He gave an exasperated sigh. "They call me Brick."

Colt gave him the once over. "Because you're built like a brick shi—"

"Can we go now?" Brick folded his arms. This only made his biceps bigger.

"Where?" I wasn't going with this Muscle Beach escapee without knowing our destination.

Brick sighed again and pointed toward the flat metal device in front of me on the table. I looked down to find it was no longer blank. A message scrolled across its impossibly thin screen.

'Brick will bring you to me. M.'

# CHAPTER FIFTY-NINE

WE LEFT Fahrenheit behind and drove for almost an hour into the wilderness to the east of Lake Tahoe, following a road that soon changed to cracked and broken asphalt. Brooks took the front seat while the rest of us sat in the back. Brick, who refused to give us his real name, remained mostly quiet. He let the car carry us into the wilds and occasionally glanced at us via the rear-view mirror. His concern was centered mostly on Clara, who peered out of the window and made occasional comments about crazies, or some other danger lurking beyond the road.

"She okay?" He asked, eventually.

"I don't know," I answered, which was the truth. "I'm hoping Professor Morecambe can tell us."

"Speaking of which," Brooks said. "Where exactly are you taking us?"

"You'll find out soon enough," came the reply. Brick never took his eyes from the road even though the car was in automatic drive mode.

"Professor Morecambe is waiting for us?"

Brick didn't answer.

"Let me guess," Brooks said with a snort. "We'll find out soon enough."

"If you know the answer, why did you ask?" Brick said.

"Beats me." Brooks lapsed back into silence.

No one spoke for the rest of the trip. At first, we were heading down out of the mountains that ringed the lake but soon leveled out into a river valley. We followed this in a northerly direction, passing the crumbling remains of civilization. Abandoned buildings dotted the landscape, many missing their roofs and windows. We soon passed through what was left of Nevada's old state capital, Carson City, which was now mostly rubble. As we passed through the derelict Main Street, littered with reminders of a time when people still called this place home, Brick finally spoke again.

"This place was thriving a hundred years ago." He pointed to a clutch of ruined structures clinging to a rise near the base of the mountains in the distance. "My family lived over there. They stayed when most other people left. Thought they could ride out the drought."

"And did they?" Colt asked.

"They don't live there no more, and I can't remember the last time it rained," Brick replied. "So what do you think?"

"Sorry to hear that," I said.

Brick merely grunted and turned his attention frontward again.

We left the remains of Carson City behind and started climbing back up into the mountains. At one point, we passed a rickety old wooden sign on the side of the road in the shadow of a vertical rock face. It was weathered and rotten after decades of exposure to the elements, but the lettering was still discernible in places. VIR—IA C—TY. 8 M—LES.

"Virginia City," Colt muttered under his breath.

I glanced toward him.

"Old mining town. Part of the real Wild West. Mark Twain called it home for a few years."

"Huh."

"Can't imagine there's much left of it now."

"A few minutes and we'll find out," Brooks said. "I can't imagine this road goes anywhere else."

And he was right. Fifteen minutes later, we rolled into town. As it turned out, Colt was also right. There wasn't much left. Mostly the foundations of buildings and weed-choked avenues where the streets had once run. Most of the structures had been made of wood, judging by the number of sun-bleached planks and timber supports lying around many of the foundations. I saw window casings. Sticks of broken furniture. The brick buildings on Main Street had fared better. But even these were mostly empty shells with boarded-up windows.

I wondered how much further it would be until we reached Professor Morecambe. It turned out we were already there. Brick turned into an alley between two abandoned buildings and drove to the back, where he parked up.

He exited the car and waited for us to climb out before motioning toward a door set into the rear of the closest building. "We're here. This is it."

"This place?" Brooks studied the dilapidated building.

"Didn't anyone ever tell you not to judge a book by its cover?" Said a voice from behind us.

I turned to see a slim young woman with flowing red hair coming toward us from the building on the other side of the alley. She wore skinny jeans and a white T-shirt that accentuated her curves. Her movements were graceful. She possessed finely sculpted features and for a moment my breath caught in my throat.

In her hand was a wrench.

"Problem?" Brick asked, narrowing his eyes.

"Power plant was playing up," the woman told him. "I fixed it."

"You should've waited for me to come back," Brick said. He didn't look pleased.

"I have three advanced degrees. I think I can handle it." The woman looked my way, and a wide smile broke out on her face. She dropped the wrench and flung her arms around me in a tight embrace. "Hayden. I can't believe you're really here. Oh, my God... I've missed you so much."

# CHAPTER SIXTY

THE INSIDE of the building was in much better condition than the exterior. We stood in a large open room that served as both the professor's work area, and her living space. One wall was taken up by what I could only describe as huge computer monitors, although they appeared more like holographic projections than solid pieces of equipment. This was confirmed when she turned them off with a terse voice command.

"Choi. Monitors off."

The screens disappeared as if they were never there.

"Choi?" I asked her, although my mind was still on the overly familiar hug she had given me outside.

"My AI assistant. The name roughly translates to keeper of the mountain. I thought it was appropriate." Morecambe turned her attention to Clara. "Brooks and Colt I know already, but who's this?"

I introduced her, although Clara showed little sign of recognizing her surroundings. Her condition, whatever that might be, was getting worse. She was mumbling under her breath, her eyes shifting wildly from one side of the room to the other. She had completely checked out, and I now wondered if she was even aware of our presence.

"What's wrong with her?" Morecambe asked.

"I was hoping you could tell me," I said.

Brooks stepped forward. "She was fine when we took her from the alternate dimension, but since then, she's been growing steadily worse. She sees things."

"crazies," I said. "People driven insane by the collapsing parallel world. There are monsters in that universe, too. She also sees them."

"Heaven knows what she's experiencing at this moment," Brooks said.

"I see." Morecambe moved close to Clara and studied her face. "How long was she in the parallel world?"

I shrugged. "Impossible to tell."

"She's a Lotto," Brooks said as if that provided the answer.

"Which parallel dimension was she in?"

"9B6."

The name meant nothing to me. I wondered if it referred to my reality being the ninth alternate world created. Or maybe the sixth. I figured it could go either way.

"Really?" Morecambe's brow furrowed. "That reality was abandoned while I was still working for the committee. She must've been in there for a couple of years, at least."

"I was in there," I said. "And according to Brooks, I was captured after you turned away from the government and came to work for One World."

"You are the one that convinced me to do that." The professor's cheeks flushed red, just a little. "Among other things."

"So I've been told," I replied, then quantified my statement. "Changing your allegiance to One World, that is. I can't comment on anything else. No memory."

"Don't worry." Morecambe's gaze shifted to me. A playful

smile touched her lips. "I'll tell you everything you want to know, but let's do that in private."

I cleared my throat. "Getting back to the point…"

"Right. 9B6 was closed down while I still worked for the government so that we could move on to 9B7. They didn't provide any explanation at the time, but I later came to realize it was because the alternate reality was unstable. If we put anyone else in it, the world's demise would be accelerated."

"So how did I end up in it?"

"Good question." Morecambe ran a hand through her lustrous red hair. "You made a lot of enemies before your capture. When they wiped your memory and sent you over, they turned you into a poster boy for the safety of alternate realities. The alternative was to kill you and make a martyr."

"Which is why they put him in that particular reality," Brooks said. "They didn't want to kill him here, but they didn't want to risk Hayden hanging around too long, either. They threw him into a reality they knew was collapsing and would do the job for them."

"That's why it took us so long to find him," Colt said.

"Almost a year," Brooks added.

"Clara was in there much longer," Morecambe said. "She was sent over during one of the Lotto rounds."

"Still doesn't tell us what's wrong with her," I said, glancing at Clara. Her hands were reaching out, grasping at thin air. And her eyes… They never stopped moving, even though no one else could see what she was looking at. "Or how to fix it."

"I think it does." Morecambe rubbed her chin. "I've seen this before. Several years ago, when we were working on the first realities."

"You have?" I couldn't keep the shock from my voice.

Morecambe nodded. "We called it Separation Syndrome. It was during the earliest trials when we wanted to make sure the realities were safe."

"You didn't do a very good job on that score," I muttered. "The reality they dumped me into was anything but safe."

"Hey. You're preaching to the converted." Morecambe stepped close to me and touched my face. Her fingers grazed my cheek. "I wish you could remember."

"Me too." I took a step back, the touch making me uncomfortable. I wondered if Clara was processing any of this on a subconscious level and what she would say if we ever got her back? Clearly, my relationship with Morecambe had been more than just professional.

"Sorry." Morecambe withdrew her hand and took a step away from me. "Old habits."

"That's okay." Even though I couldn't remember my real life, the connection between us was undeniable. But then there was Clara... "About Separation Syndrome?"

"Right." Morecambe paced toward the monitor wall. Instructed her AI to activate the screens again. "We left people in the original reality for six months, then withdrew them. We weren't expecting any issues, but within a week of their return, each of them started to display symptoms similar to Clara."

Morecambe played a video for us. It showed a man in his forties. He was in a small white room devoid of furniture. He walked in circles, his hands reaching for invisible objects. The man mumbled and looked from side to side. At intervals, his voice grew loud, and he shouted as if arguing with an unseen companion.

"This is one of the people you pulled back?" I asked.

"Yes."

"You said they were only in that dimension for six months. I was in the alternate reality for longer than that, and I'm not showing any signs of this affliction."

"That's because we were able to tweak the process. We got to the point where a person could cross over for a certain time without adverse effects. But we could never wipe out the syndrome entirely. Once a subject had been in the alternate dimension for more than a year, the chances of them developing Separation Syndrome rose significantly. After eighteen months on the other side, pretty much every subject brought back developed it."

"What happened to them after that?" I asked, not sure I wanted to know the answer.

"They couldn't separate from the other dimension. Their mind was operating in two places at once. They couldn't sustain that for long," Morecambe said. "Within a few weeks of their return, every one of them died."

# CHAPTER SIXTY-ONE

"You've got to be kidding." If what Professor Morecambe claimed was true, Clara's condition would only get worse until . . . It didn't bear thinking about. "Is there anything you can do?"

"To reverse her syndrome?" Morecambe shook her head. "I'm afraid not. At least, if you want her to stay in this reality."

"What does that mean?" I asked.

"Simple. If we put her back into the same reality from which she came quickly enough, she might stand a chance of surviving. If she stays here, she won't live more than another week or two."

"That's it?" The situation was hopeless. "We either let her die here or put her back into a collapsing dimension?"

"Yes." Morecambe turned the monitors back off. "I know that's not what you want to hear."

"Even if we wanted to put her back into that dimension, we can't," Brooks said. "The machine you built with Hayden back in Refuge City is gone. Destroyed."

"So I hear," Morecambe said. "And you are all fugitives. Terrorists no less."

"We didn't blow up our own headquarters," Brooks said.

"Obviously not. Won't stop them coming after you, though."

"The authorities have been on our tail ever since the explosion. We were set up. Senator Kane."

"I never trusted her," Morecambe said. "Even when I worked for the government. She was a snake. No morals, that one."

"She also saved our hides after that dust storm," Colt said. "We wouldn't be here if she hadn't helped us."

"Still doesn't mean I trust her," Brooks said. "Just because she claims to be back on our side doesn't mean she really is."

"You accepted her ride."

"Because we had no choice. And because I knew that once we reached Fahrenheit, our trail would go cold. Whatever she's up to, the senator can't find us here."

"I hope you're right," Morecambe said. She walked to a large metal cabinet in her work area, opened it, and removed a handheld device that looked a bit like a digital thermometer. She approached Clara and pressed it against her neck. There was a slight sound like escaping air. When she withdrew the device, the skin underneath was red. "That should help Clara in the short term."

"What did you do to her?" I asked.

"I injected her with a neuron inhibitor. Basically, it's a soup of nanobots that will block the signals she's receiving from the other dimension. It will last a couple of days at most, but in the meantime, she'll have some relief."

"She won't see those creatures from the other dimension?"

"That's right. Give it an hour or two and she should be back to herself, at least temporarily."

"How does it work?" I asked.

"I could spend all day answering that, and you probably wouldn't understand a word of it unless you're a neuroscientist. The short answer is that there's a small structure inside the brain called the claustrum. It sits below the cerebral cortex and acts as a transducer. Basically, it converts a signal from one form into another. In this case, that signal is consciousness. With me so far?"

"Not really," I said. Even the short version was confusing.

"Let me see if I can make it clear," Morecambe replied. "For centuries, millennia even, scientists and philosophers grappled with the notion of consciousness. Where did it come from? Why did we need it as biological units? Eventually, it became clear that consciousness was a force of nature, much like gravity. It does not reside within the brain but is received *by the brain* in the same way that radios would pick up signals back in the day and convert them into sound. When Clara was put into the alternate dimension, that signal changed to accommodate her new environment."

"Much like re-tuning a radio to a different station," I said.

"A basic analogy, but it works."

"And when we brought her back, she didn't quite tune back to the original station," I said, starting to understand.

"Right. Her brain is trying to receive signals from two different dimensions simultaneously. At first, she could compensate for this, but then her brain started to lose the battle."

"There's no way to fix her permanently?"

"I'm afraid not. The nanobots will work for a while, but as the condition worsens, they won't be able to compensate."

"Which leaves us back at square one," Brooks said.

"Not necessarily," I said to Brooks. "Professor Morecambe and I built a machine that could move people between dimensions once. We can do so again."

"Did you forget that the dimension is collapsing?" Brooks asked.

"No. But it will buy us some time to figure this out," I turned to Morecambe. "Isn't that right?"

"Hayden. You can call me Belinda," Morecambe said,

that same red flush tinging her cheeks. "We're not exactly strangers."

"I beg to differ," I said. "To me, you really are a stranger right now."

"How about you call me Belinda anyway," Morecambe said, a look of hurt flashing across her face before she stifled it.

"Very well. Belinda."

"That's better. And yes, Clara would be safe in the other dimension, at least until it collapses." Morecambe folded her arms. "But it's not that easy. Rebuilding the machine will take time and resources we don't have. It took us two months to build the machine last time, and we had better access to parts. Clara doesn't have that long."

"We've already done it once. It should be easier a second time around." I was grasping at any glimmer of hope, no matter how faint.

"Hayden, it's not about that. I have an eidetic memory. I know how to put that machine together. But we still need the components at hand and the time to assemble them. We have neither of those things."

"There's nothing we can do, then?"

"I'm afraid not," Morecambe said. "But in the meantime, Clara must rest so the nanobots can do their job. I have guestrooms on the second level. Enough for each of you. This place used to be a hotel. I'm sure you're all tired after such a long journey."

"We are," Brooks said.

"In that case, Brick will take you up before he leaves for the evening."

"He doesn't live here with you?" Colt asked.

"No. He has his own accommodation further down the mountain. We both prefer it that way." Morecambe turned her attention to me. "I'll stop by and see you once you've rested, and we'll talk. We have a lot of catching up to do."

"Sure." I nodded and glanced at Clara, who was still as spaced out as before. I hoped the nanobots worked soon, although I wasn't sure what I would tell her when they did. She was dying, and there was no way to save her.

# CHAPTER SIXTY-TWO

CLARA WAS SLEEPING. It was two hours later, and I was on the second floor of Professor Morecambe's old hotel building in one of the bedrooms provided to us. Colt and Brooks were across the hall, while I had my own room next door to Clara. I didn't set Brick straight when he showed us our accommodations. Morecambe did not know we were an item, and I felt it should remain that way for now given the obvious vibes I was getting from the professor.

I sat on the edge of Clara's bed and watched her, hoping the nanobots were restoring her sanity while she slept. I missed her already and dreaded what I knew was coming. Even if Professor Morecambe's little robots helped Clara, the effects would be short term. She would soon slip back into the same semi-lucid state that had descended upon her after we reached Fahrenheit. After that, it would be downhill until her body and mind could no longer cope with the duality of her existence. Stuck straddling two realities, the time would come when there wasn't enough of her left in either one to keep her alive.

The implications of this for Darwin had not escaped me.

Even if we were able to reconstruct the machine, we could not bring Darwin back to this reality. He must have been in the alternate universe for at least as long as Clara. That meant he was bonded with it and would soon lose his mind, just as Clara had, if we removed him.

I took Clara's hand, closed my eyes, and said a silent prayer. I didn't know if anyone was listening out there in the cold, dark universe, but I hoped so.

There was a light knock at the door.

I placed Clara's hand gently back on the bed and went to the door. Professor Morecambe was standing on the other side.

"I figured you would be watching over her," she said.

I shrugged. "She's been sleeping ever since we came up here."

"That's because the nanobots are trying to disengage her brain from the dual realities. Give her time. She'll wake up, and when she does, she will feel so much better."

"I hope so," I said, keeping my voice low so I wouldn't disturb Clara.

"Can we talk?"

"Isn't that what we're doing right now?"

"No. I mean in private. Just you and me." Morecambe glanced toward the pair of rooms Brooks and Colt occupied. Their doors were closed and there was no sound from within. They were probably sleeping too.

"I'm not sure I should leave Clara alone."

"She'll be fine for a while, trust me. She probably won't even wake up." Morecambe hesitated, stared into my eyes. Again, she reached out and touched my face, the contact brief and light. "God, I can't believe you're actually here, that it's really you."

"It is."

"Yes. It really is." Morecambe stepped back. "Let's go for

a walk. I won't keep you away from her for long. Promise. I know you're worried."

"Okay, then." I glanced back toward Clara to make sure she was still asleep, then stepped into the corridor and pulled the door closed. "Lead the way."

# CHAPTER SIXTY-THREE

MORECAMBE TOOK me downstairs and through the building to what must have been the hotel bar back in the day. Most of its fixtures were still there, reminding me of something from an old Western movie. The room was mostly empty save for a line of stools pulled up to the bar. The floor was dusty and unswept. Damask wallpaper, once bright red and printed with a swirling repeating motif that looked French to my eyes, was peeling from the walls in places. Several bottles of liquor sat on a low shelf behind a mirrored back bar that was now tarnished and struggling to reflect the light.

Morecambe moved behind the bar and grabbed a bottle. "Bourbon. It was always your favorite."

"I'll have to take your word for that," I replied. "Guess I'm more of a craft beer man these days."

"You'll have a bourbon." Morecambe pulled two glasses out and poured a measure into each. "Best I can do."

"Fair enough." I took my glass and looked down into the amber liquid. The fumes hit my nose and reminded me of happier times with friends hanging out in bars back in Burlington. It felt like another lifetime, and perhaps it was.

Morecambe observed me for a few moments and took a swig of her own drink. She smacked her lips. "That's better."

I looked around, noting the dilapidated state of our surroundings. "Where do you even get this stuff up here?"

"Brick finds it for me. He has contacts back east. Comes in on the monthly supply run to Fahrenheit." Morecambe set her glass on the counter. "What happened to you in that other world, Hayden?"

"I wrote a book."

"Really?" Morecambe smirked. "Don't suppose you have a copy."

"It wasn't high on my list of things to grab when the world went to hell." I still hadn't touched my drink. I wanted to keep a clear head.

"I get that." Morecambe leaned on the bar. "I still can't believe you're here. I never thought I would see you again."

I still had the flat credit card device in my pocket. I pulled it out and laid it on the bar. "Some small part of you must have thought I would make it back, or you wouldn't have given this to Brooks before you disappeared."

"My original plan was to stay and look for you, but the authorities were closing in. If I hadn't gone underground, I would have ended up the same as you, or worse."

"They really would have killed you?"

"Still want to, I'm sure." Morecambe picked up the device. "This was a long shot. I encoded the message but it but never really expected anything to come of this."

I thought about the message appearing on the impossibly thin screen back at the safe house after the card scanned my identity. "Did you know I was back from the moment I activated it?"

"No. The card doesn't notify me until it's within a certain distance of my location. I built that in as a proportion in case it fell into the wrong hands. Wouldn't want the authorities tracing me back here."

"It notified you when we entered Fahrenheit."

"Correct. It was quite a shock. I wasn't expecting it."

"And then you sent Brick to get us."

Morecambe nodded. "Even then, I didn't really believe it. I thought it more likely that either Brooks or the authorities had tracked me down… Then Brick confirmed it was you."

"In the flesh," I said.

"And Clara?" Morecambe finished her drink and poured another one. "What's her deal?"

"You know what her deal is. She went over to the alternate universe after winning a lottery."

"The Great Migration."

"Exactly. Although I'm not sure winning would be the right word when you end up killed by that same collapsing universe."

"That doesn't answer my question," Morecambe said.

"You mean the deal between me and her," I said.

"You clearly care for her. Are you in a relationship?" Morecambe studied my face as she asked that question.

"How about you answer a question for me first," I said.

"Shoot."

"Were we in a relationship before I got sent over to the other universe?"

"What do you think?"

"I have a feeling that we were," I replied. "Although maybe I'm just way off base."

"You're not," Morecambe said, a wistful note in her voice. "We kept it on the lowdown. Thought it would be better that way. I'm sure Brooks suspected, though."

"If he did, he hasn't mentioned it."

Morecambe nodded. "Your turn. Tell me about Clara."

"Not sure what you want me to say. We met when our world went haywire and we stuck together. We were friends at first, but it became something more."

"Do you love her?"

I didn't want to answer that because I might once have been in love with the woman asking the question. A woman and relationship I no longer remembered. If I was honest with myself, a small part of me remembered what we had. But not intellectually. This was more like muscle memory. I didn't wish to hurt her.

My hesitation did not go unnoticed.

"Your silence appears to confirm my suspicion."

"Professor Morecambe..." I caught myself. "Belinda. I have no recollection of our time together. I wish I did. But I'm not the same person you knew back then."

"Yes, you are. That's why this is so hard." Morecambe looked at the bottle of bourbon. "Here I am contemplating my third glass, and you haven't even touched your first."

I pushed my drink across the bar. "Take it."

"I'd better not." She studied me with a look somewhere between love and sadness.

It made me uncomfortable. "You asked me to take a walk with you."

"I did."

"Let's do it then," I said, even though I really wanted to check on Clara.

"Maybe later." Morecambe returned the bourbon bottle to the shelf. She smiled, but I knew it was a mask. "You should go back upstairs."

# CHAPTER SIXTY-FOUR

CLARA WAS STILL SLEEPING when I went back upstairs, so I retired to my room and lay on the bed. I must have fallen asleep because when I awoke, it was dark outside. I rose and went next door to Clara's room. There was a lamp in the corner which I turned on at its lowest setting. It filled the room with soft yellow light. Just enough to see by.

I crossed to the bed and sat down. At first, I thought Clara was still out of it, but then she sat up.

"Hayden. I wondered where you were," she said in a sleepy voice.

"I was just next door. I came to check on you."

"I'm fine." Clara smiled, but I could tell there wasn't much enthusiasm behind it. "I must've been pretty out of it, huh?"

"That's putting it mildly," I said. "You remember anything?"

"Bits and pieces. But it felt like a really vivid dream. We were in Fahrenheit, and we were driving up here. But at the same time, I was in the other dimension and there were monsters and crazies and all sorts of bad things."

"What else do you remember?"

"Well, for one, that red-haired woman giving you a big old hug."

"You saw that, huh?"

"Yeah. I saw it. Care to explain?"

"I'm not sure I can. The professor and I appear to have been close in my previous existence."

"Does she still think that you are?"

"I think she harbored a hope," I said, then added quickly, "Which I shot down."

"I should hope so." Clara paused, a thoughtful look passing across her face. "What happened to me after that?"

"The professor gave you an injection of nanobots. Said it would clear your head, at least temporarily."

"Nanobots. Really?" Clara bit her bottom lip. "And what happens when those temporary effects wear off?"

"Let's not worry about that right now," I said, trying to steer her away from that topic of conversation.

"Because I won't like the answer, correct?"

"Something like that. You're suffering from an affliction called Separation Syndrome. It's something about your brain getting stuck in two realities at the same time. The only permanent cure would be to go back into the other universe."

"Hardly a great solution since it's collapsing and is about to kill everyone inside of it," Clara said.

"I wouldn't worry too much. It's not a possibility. The professor said it would take too long to rebuild the machine."

Clara let this sink in. "Answer me this. If we brought Darwin back from that collapsing universe, would he end up with this syndrome too?"

"Yes. The more time you spend there, the more likely you are to get it."

"So even if we could rebuild the machine in time and find Darwin, our choice would be to stay in the other universe which would cure the Separation Syndrome but kill us when it collapses or come to this world and end up stuck between two planes of existence."

"That's pretty much it."

"And the Separation Syndrome. Will it kill us?"

Hayden nodded.

Clara processed this for a moment, then said, "Not much of a choice."

"It's not a choice at all. We don't have a machine." I hated saying this, but it was the truth.

"I don't want to think about it anymore," said Clara. "My mind is clear and I'm not seeing crazies and monsters. That's good enough for tonight."

"I just have one question," I said, hoping I wasn't pushing her too far. "When you *were seeing them*, was it worse?"

"Was what worse?"

"Then when we were there. Your affliction... it was a window into that other world. What you were seeing wasn't a hallucination. It was real."

"And you want to know how bad it's gotten in our world. The one we still think of as home."

I nodded.

Clara took a deep breath. "Yes. It's worse. The crazies are everywhere, and there were a lot of monsters. And not just the ones we ran into when we were trying to reach New Haven. There are other things now. Worse things."

"I find that hard to believe."

"So do I, but it's true." Clara took my hand. "I really don't want to talk about this right now."

"Okay. Sorry." Maybe I had pushed her too far. "Not another word."

"Good. Get undressed and climb on in with me." She flipped the covers back. "Come on."

"You sure? Bed's pretty small."

"Just get in here," Clara said. "Unless you're worried about upsetting Professor Morecambe, of course."

"Not worried about that at all." I stood and peeled off my shirt.

"Good." Clara watched me undress. When I was done, she shifted over to make room. "Because she can't have you. At least, not while I still have half a mind."

"Not funny," I said, climbing in next to her.

She wrapped her arms around me. "It wasn't meant to be."

# CHAPTER SIXTY-FIVE

I awoke in the darkness to a high-pitched wail.

Beside me, Clara stirred. "What's that?"

"Don't know. Sounds like a siren. It can't be good." I jumped out of bed and turned on the light. After pulling on my clothes, I went to the door.

When I cracked the door open and looked out into the corridor, Brooks was already there. He wore a pair of jeans and was pulling a tee over his head.

"You know what's going on?" Brooks asked.

"About as much as you," I replied as the noise shut off.

"That's better," Brooks said. "Could hardly hear myself think."

"We should find the professor, get some answers," I said.

"Good idea, but let's not take any chances. Get your gun." Brooks was already ducking back into his room.

I did the same.

Clara was getting dressed, a worried expression on her face. "Does Brooks know what's happening?"

"No." I looked around for the gun, didn't see it leaning against the wall by the door, where I had left it earlier. "Did you move the rifle?"

"No." Clara finished buttoning her top.

"It's not where I left it," I said, puzzled. A quick search of the room proved fruitless.

When I stepped back into the corridor, Brooks looked just as concerned. "My rifle is gone."

"Mine too." I glanced toward the closed bedroom door next to the room Brooks occupied. "Where's Colt?"

"Good question." I went to his door and knocked. There was no answer. I tried the handle. The door was unlocked. I stepped inside and looked around. The room was empty.

Brooks followed me inside. "I don't like this."

"Me either." I turned to step past Brooks, back into the corridor.

Clara was standing in the doorway. She pointed toward the window. "Look."

I turned toward the window, which faced the road we had driven up on. It had an unobstructed view over the roof of the one-story building next door. Even in the darkness, I could make out the road snaking out of town and disappearing down the mountainside.

But Clara wasn't interested in the road. She was looking at a ball of orange flame that belched up into the night sky from further down the mountain.

A moment later, the rumble of an explosion reached our ears.

"Let's find the others," Brooks said, racing toward the door. "We need to get some answers."

"Right behind you." I followed Brooks out into the corridor with Clara at my heel. We made our way downstairs to the hotel's old lounge area that doubled as both a living space and Belinda Morecambe's office.

The professor was already there, standing at her desk and looking at the holographic monitors above. When we entered, she turned to us. "Proximity sensors on the road below us have been tripped. There are soldiers coming."

"Shit." Brooks grimaced. "We've been found."

"It would appear so." Morecambe ran her hands over an interface on the desk. The view on the screens changed to show the road below us and the origin of the fire ball we had witnessed upstairs. A destroyed building, consumed by flames. "They killed Brick."

"Damn," Brooks said. "I kinda liked him."

"Me too," replied Morecambe, her voice laced with sadness.

"Where are the soldiers now?" I asked, all too aware that we were unarmed and vulnerable.

"Ten minutes away, maybe fifteen."

The screen changed again to show another view of the road from higher up. There were three vehicles moving through the darkness. Even though they looked more high-tech than anything I'd ever seen before, it wasn't hard to identify them. Troop carriers.

"I don't get it," I said. "No one followed us and the pilots that flew us here didn't know our final destination. We were careful."

"Not careful enough," Brooks said. "Think about it. There's only one person who could have turned us in."

"Colt."

"That doesn't make sense," I said, hoping Brooks was wrong. "He's been with us all along the way."

"You think he's gone?" Clara asked, looking around nervously.

"Maybe." Brooks swallowed. "We have to get out of here right now."

"Brick took the car back to his house further down the mountain," Morecambe said. "But there's an old truck that I keep hidden inside one of the buildings a few blocks away. Don't use it much, but Brick keeps it in running condition just in case."

"Good enough for me," Brooks said. He turned toward the door at the back of the building. "Let's go."

"Not so fast," a voice said from behind us.

I turned to see Colt standing there, with one of the rifles pointed in our direction. The pistol and the other rifle were nowhere in sight.

There was a moment of stunned silence. I exchanged a glance with Brooks, summing up our chances of taking Colt down.

Colt shook his head and tapped the gun. "I wouldn't do that. You won't even make it halfway. Now, how about you all step away from the desk and we'll hang out here for a few minutes longer. Just until those soldiers arrive…"

# CHAPTER SIXTY-SIX

"We trusted you," Brooks growled, his face red. "What the hell do you think you're doing?"

"What no one else could." Colt kept the gun leveled on us. "Killing Hayden Stone and delivering Belinda Morecambe back where she belongs."

"I'm not going anywhere with you," snapped Morecambe, anger flashing in her eyes.

"Don't be so naïve. By the time the senator has finished with you, you'll willingly work for us again."

"They're going to wipe my mind." Morecambe went pale.

"I don't know what they will do with you. Not up to me. But I guarantee it won't be pleasant."

"I don't get it," I said. "If your plan was to kill me, why didn't you just do it?" You've had plenty of opportunities."

"That's true." Colt nodded. "I was going to kill all three of you back in the safe house. But then, before I got the chance, Brooks gave you that message from Morecambe. That changed everything. I figured it was better to let the situation play out. After all, if I could lead Senator Kane to the professor even better. The multi-verse project Senate

Committee was never entirely sure she was dead despite the excellent job she did of faking it. They just didn't know where to look. They wanted her back, though. Real bad. She was the best mind they ever had."

"And now I've led our enemies right to her," I said.

"And for that, you have my gratitude."

"I don't get it," said Clara, probably buying us time. "The drones in the forest almost killed us. And we were forced to flee Happenstance in the middle of the night because government agents showed up. If you were letting things ride so we could lead you to Morecambe, what was the deal with that?"

"Simple. The senator didn't know about Morecambe. She just wanted to finish the job after you escaped that warehouse in the Packing District. Hayden had a tracker implanted in him. That's why the drones showed up." Colt looked at Brooks. "Likewise, in Happenstance. You reached out to your underworld contacts, and they had already sold you out. They were playing both sides against each other. Until we reached Happenstance, I had no way to get a message through to anyone. I couldn't risk blowing my cover. When I finally told the senator what was going on, she called off the dogs and allowed you to escape."

"I thought we got away too easy," grumbled Brooks.

"Me too." I agreed. Then I realized something else. "When our car got destroyed in the dust storm, the senator didn't show up because she had a change of heart and wanted to help us, did she? It was your doing. When I caught you outside that barn in the middle of the night, it wasn't a bathroom break. You were talking to the senator and concocting a plan to keep our journey going. You needed me to come here because it was the only way to flush out Professor Morecambe."

"Exactly." Colt smiled. "And any minute now, those soldiers will arrive and take care of you all. Just like they took care of that Neanderthal, Brick."

"Why would you do this?" Brooks asked. "And don't give me any bullshit about being coerced into helping the senator, because I won't believe it."

"There was no coercion. I wasn't being forced to do this." Colt laughed. "The senator reached out to me a few months ago, convinced me I was on the wrong side. Asked me to help her. Made me see the possibilities for my life if I did. She wanted someone on the inside. So I kept my head down, pretended I was still a loyal soldier for the cause and bided my time."

"They bought you."

"That's one way to put it. But hey, if it's any consolation, I'll be sitting on a tropical beach and enjoying the view while you're rotting in your graves."

"It's not."

Colt shrugged.

"Did you plant that bomb in our building?" Brooks asked.

"No. But I made sure the people who did plant it had the access they needed."

"You're an animal." Clara lunged forward before I could stop her. "You killed all those people."

Colt brought the gun around and fired a single shot.

At the same time, I saw movement from the corner of my eye. A large shape that lunged from the shadows behind Colt and slammed into him. It was Brick.

The sudden attack ruined Colt's aim. The shot smacked into the floor at Clara's feet as the weapon went flying.

The two men tumbled to the ground, grappling to gain the upper hand. But Brick was heavier and stronger. He maneuvered himself on top of Colt, lifted a fist, and brought it down into the man's face.

Bone cracked.

Colt let out a muffled cry.

Brick delivered a powerful roundhouse with his other arm that snapped colt's head to the side.

After that, it was over.

Brick climbed from Colt's limp body and wiped his hands on his pants. Then he looked at us. "Soldiers will be here any moment. At least thirty of them, probably more. We need to go. Right now!"

# CHAPTER SIXTY-SEVEN

"Brick. Oh my God. I thought you were dead," Morecambe said.

"I almost was," Brick replied, picking up the discarded rifle. "Got out just in time and hightailed it up here."

"Thank goodness you did," the professor said, glancing toward Colt's limp body.

"Didn't feel right when I got here, so I snuck in." Brick motioned toward Colt. "And a good thing too. I saw this scumbag holding you hostage."

I turned to Clara. "That's why you lunged at Colt."

Clara nodded. "I saw Brick hiding back there. Figured our only chance was a distraction."

"You could have been killed."

"But I wasn't." Clara grinned.

"We don't have time for this," Brooks said, turning his attention to Brick. "Do you have the car?"

"Yes." Brick nodded.

"Then what are we waiting for?" Morecambe said, heading toward the door.

At that moment, there was a boom from the front of the old hotel, forceful enough to shake the building.

Brick grabbed the professor and dragged her back. "Too late. They're here. I barricaded the door, but it didn't do any good. They've breached the front. There will be more soldiers coming around the back. I guarantee it."

"Then we're trapped," Clara said, a note of panic in her voice.

"Not necessarily." Professor Morecambe ran to her desk and opened the drawer, took out a steel box then turned back to us. "Come with me."

"Where are we going?" I asked as she led us through the back of the hotel and down a narrow corridor.

"You'll see." She moved fast and didn't look back, even though I could hear voices behind us now. The men sent by Senator Kane to kill us, and capture Morecambe, were inside the building.

Up ahead, at the end of the corridor, was a rock wall with a steel door set into it. The professor leaned close to a panel next to the door, no doubt a security system, and soon we were on the other side.

It was an adit. A horizontal mine entrance.

"Is this another way out?" I asked, surprised.

"No." The professor shook her head. "There might have been other tunnels leading to the surface back in the day, but if so, I don't know where they are."

"Then why are we here?" I couldn't imagine this would make our situation any better. We would end up trapped like rabbits in the burrow.

"Have a little faith." Morecambe grabbed a flashlight from a hook next to the door and then she was on the move again.

Brick pulled the door closed and locked it from the inside. "This will hold them, but not for long."

"I hope the professor knows what she's doing," I said to him as we followed her deeper into the mine.

"She's doing the only thing possible to save your lives."

That didn't fill me with hope.

We reached another door. This one looked like it should have been in a bank vault. It was constructed of thick metal. There was a wheel on the door to disengage the locks.

"No high-tech wizardry here?" I asked.

"Sometimes high-tech can be a disadvantage. There isn't a system in the world that can't be hacked," Morecambe replied. "This is old-school. No electronics."

She spun the wheel. Brooks and I stepped forward and helped her heave the door open. It was light on its hinges, considering it must have been at least a foot thick.

We hurried past the door and into a chamber hewn out of solid rock. In the middle stood a piece of equipment that I recognized from the skyscraper back in Refuge City. A round platform with a circular portal attached, big enough for a person to step through. It was a machine identical to the one that had transported us out of the alternate universe.

"What the hell?" I could hardly believe my eyes. "You had this all along and didn't tell us?"

"I wanted to, but I didn't know who to trust," Morecambe said. "And it seems I was right to have my reservations, given what just happened with Colt. Except for you, Hayden. I trusted you."

"This is what you were going to show me last night when you said we should take a walk," I said, the pieces clicking into place.

"Yes. But when I realized you love Clara, I decided not to. I didn't want to put you in the impossible situation of having to choose how she dies."

Clara looked our way, startled by the conversation, but said nothing.

"You still should have told me about it. It wasn't your decision to make." I said, glaring at the professor.

"You're right. I probably should have told you."

"Why is this even here?" I asked, staring at the machine.

"I was using it to look for you." Morecambe put the metal

case on a small table next to the machine and opened it. Inside were six bracelets that looked like the ones Brooks had given us to escape the alternate universe days before. "Built it as soon as I came here."

"Some help would be appreciated." Brick was at the door, heaving it closed. I could see uniformed men with guns racing toward us in the mine tunnel beyond. One of them lifted a weapon and fired without breaking stride. The bullet pinged on the metal door inches from Brick's head.

I rushed over to him. Brooks did the same. We slammed the door closed and engaged the inner locks a moment before a volley of gunfire hit the door's outer skin.

"That should hold them for a little while," Brick said. "I've disengaged the opening mechanism on the other side."

"Is there another way out of here?" I asked, looking around.

"Just one," Morecambe said, handing a bracelet to each of us. Behind her, the machine was humming to life. A bright white light filled the circular portal, masking the wall behind. It rippled and shimmered, like a cascading waterfall.

"Is this safe?" I asked, looking down at the bracelet.

"Does it matter?" Morecambe replied. Loud metallic bangs were coming from the other side of the steel door—raised voices. The soldiers were trying to break through. "If we stay here, we'll all die."

# CHAPTER SIXTY-EIGHT

It wasn't much of a choice. Stay and wait for the men on the other side of the door to gain entrance to the chamber we were trapped in, or step into a machine that would transport us to a failing universe.

I turned to Morecambe. "Have you got a plan beyond stepping into that thing?"

"I'm not sure I'd call it a plan. At least, not a fully formed one." Morecambe glanced toward the door as a loud bang echoed from the tunnel beyond. "But there's no time to explain right now. They're using explosives. That door won't last much longer."

"Hayden." Clara gripped my arm. "I'd rather go back to our world than stand here waiting to be killed. At least we have a chance there."

"Not much of one," I said.

"Better than certain death." Brooks slipped one of the bracelets on and activated it. He walked to the machine, glanced back at us, then stepped up onto the platform. He glanced at Morecambe. "You got any idea what to expect on the other side?"

"No," she answered. "Except that it's the world you found Hayden in."

"Still better than a bullet in the head," Brooks said. Then he stepped forward into the portal. The shimmering light flowed around him. Enveloped him. For a moment, he remained visible as a translucent ghostly form until the light swallowed him up and Brooks vanished.

"Next person," Morecambe said, looking at Clara. "You. And remember, hold your breath. Whatever you do, don't breathe on the way across. Understand?"

"Yes. Just like before," Clara said, hesitating. She turned to me. Her face was pale. "See you on the other side."

I nodded.

Clara mounted the platform and was soon gone.

Morecambe motioned for me to go next.

I shook my head. "You go first."

Morecambe looked like she wanted to argue but thought better of it. Perhaps she really did know me. She approached the portal, drew a big breath, and stepped through.

"Now you," I said to brick.

He shook his head. "I'm staying."

"Don't be ridiculous." I couldn't believe what I was hearing. "They will kill you."

"Perhaps. But someone has to stay and disable the machine, otherwise those soldiers can just follow us through."

"Not if they don't have bracelets," I said.

"And how long do you think it will take them to find some?" Brick gave me a shove toward the portal. "We can't let them know where you went. Which universe."

"Won't they figure that out anyway?"

"Maybe. Maybe not. Either way, they won't be right on your tail."

I hated leaving him there, but there wasn't time to argue. "Good luck."

"Right back at you." Brick raised the rifle. "I'll take as many of them with me as I can. Tell the professor goodbye."

"I will," I said, then made my way onto the platform, took a deep breath, and stepped into the shimmering light.

# CHAPTER SIXTY-NINE

THE JOURNEY back to the reality I thought of as home was no better than the trip out of it. Despite the shimmering white light inside the portal, the netherworld between dimensions was a black swirling void that stretched out endlessly into oblivion. Like before, I held my breath and struggled not to cry out as I was pulled from one timeline to another. Pain lit up every fiber of my being. It flowed through me like a current. I closed my eyes and clenched my teeth.

And then it was over.

The void was gone, replaced by warm sunlight.

I stumbled and almost fell, gasping for breath.

Brooks caught me. "Easy there. Try to relax."

"Relax? You've got to be kidding. I swear that was worse than last time."

"Where's Brick?" asked Morecambe after a few seconds passed. "He should be right behind you."

"He's not coming," I said.

"I thought as much," Morecambe replied without asking why.

"He told me to say goodbye."

Morecambe nodded but said nothing, perhaps contemplating the fate that awaited her friend.

From behind us, there was a flash and sharp bang. The air sizzled with electricity. The portal had closed for good. Brick had destroyed it on the other side.

"Where are we exactly?" Clara asked.

That was a good question. I looked around. We were standing on a street surrounded by three and four-story buildings. There were cars parked along each side of the road. But not the sleek driverless cars of the world Brooks had brought us to. These cars were different. Familiar. Our surroundings felt familiar too, although I couldn't quite place them until the professor spoke up.

"Long Island. Queens, to be precise," Morecambe said. "It's one of the places my machine likes to dump me. I've traveled to this world more than fifty times, and in at least half those trips, I end up in Queens. Don't ask me why."

"New York," Clara said. "I can't believe it. This is New York City."

"It's better than that," I said, putting my arms around her. "It's home. We're back where we belong."

Printed in Great Britain
by Amazon

38494425R00162